"Alyssa, all you have to do is hold on to me and I'll get us out of this."

She shook her head. Her blue eyes didn't drop their stare. It finally clicked in place for Caleb. He should have realized why she was so terrified.

An overwhelming wave of feeling surged through him. Without a second thought he angled her face up. Then he met her mouth with his own.

The kiss was meant to distract Alyssa from her fear, to give her something else to focus on. Caleb also hoped it reminded her that he was there, down in the trenches with her. That, no matter what, he'd get her to safety.

Yet all thoughts and intentions fell away as the warmth of Alyssa's lips pressed against his. Those pink, pink lips aroused something almost primal in Caleb. He wanted it to last. He wanted her...

THE DEPUTY'S WITNESS

TYLER ANNE SNELL

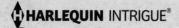

HARLEQUIN INTRIGUE®

Recycling programs
for this product may
not exist in your area.

ISBN-13: 978-1-335-72142-6

The Deputy's Witness

Copyright © 2017 by Tyler Anne Snell

Printed in U.S.A.

Tyler Anne Snell genuinely loves all genres of the written word. However, she's realized that she loves books filled with sexual tension and mysteries a little more than the rest. Her stories have a good dose of both. Tyler lives in Alabama with her same-named husband and their mini "lions." When she isn't reading or writing, she's playing video games and working on her blog, *Almost There*. To follow her shenanigans, visit tylerannesnell.com.

Books by Tyler Anne Snell

Harlequin Intrigue

The Protectors of Riker County

Small-Town Face-Off
The Deputy's Witness

Orion Security

Private Bodyguard
Full Force Fatherhood
Be on the Lookout: Bodyguard
Suspicious Activities

Manhunt

CAST OF CHARACTERS

Deputy Caleb Foster—A routine call gets him transferred from Portland to Riker County, but all he can think about is leaving. It isn't until he meets a witness for a local bank robbery trial that he realizes he'll have to make a choice. Will he keep his head down or will he put everything on the line to keep the Alabama beauty safe?

Alyssa Garner—She's ready to take the stand and serve justice to a group of bank robbers so she can move on with her life. But someone else has different plans. After a chance encounter with a handsome new deputy, Alyssa knows her life isn't about to return to normal. She's not willing to let the guilty go unpunished, but can she trust a man who can't wait to leave town?

Robbie and Eleanor Rickman—A former bank security guard and his wife. This couple becomes as close as family to Alyssa after the robbery.

Dante Mills—Assigned as Caleb's partner, this deputy's refusal to stay away from the loner earns him the spot of trusted friend.

The Storm Chasers—Nicknamed for using a storm to cover their actions, this group of three orchestrates a bank robbery that shakes the town to its very core.

Captain Dane Jones—He may not like Caleb's methods but he'll do whatever he can to keep Alyssa and their county safe.

Chapter One

The rain slapped the windshield in such fierce bursts that Alyssa Garner almost decided not to go into the bank at all.

She moved her glasses up to the bridge of her nose and peered out the window, analyzing the few feet between her car door and the overhang of the Waller Street Credit Union's awning. If she used the two-week-old *Carpenter Times* she'd thrown on the back seat floorboard as a makeshift umbrella, she might not get soaked to the bone.

Alyssa looked down at her outfit. She worked at Jeffries & Sons Remodeling, and apart from being the only employee who was not a Jeffries, she was the only one who ran the day-to-day operations pertaining to the physical office. That meant she was the first person anyone saw when they walked through the front door. Even though she wasn't a Jeffries or a son, she played a big part in creating a first impression of the small business. Which meant she was currently wearing a finely pressed white blouse, a pencil skirt and black heels that boosted her height considerably. An outfit that didn't match with the downpour outside.

She sucked on her bottom lip, considering the option of forgoing the bank run until the next day. But just as quickly as she had the thought, she sighed, defeated. While corporations and bigger businesses might be able to push off making weighty deposits by just one day, places like Jeffries couldn't afford the delay. Alyssa took her cell phone out of her purse and slid it between the waist of her skirt and her stomach. Some women couldn't go anywhere without their purses. Alyssa was that way about her phone. She blamed her sister, Gabby, for that. Whenever Alyssa pointed out that Gabby always had her phone, her little sister would snap back with a simple, yet effective stance.

"The one time you don't have it is the one time you'll need it the most."

It was hard to argue with logic like that.

Alyssa adjusted the phone against her so it wasn't noticeable, put the deposit bag beneath one arm and grabbed the newspaper. Thunder crashed loudly overhead, but Alyssa crossed the divide between her car and the bank's front door without getting swept away in the storm.

However, her glasses fogged the moment the wet air pressed against her. She paused in front of the glass double door to take them off before walking inside. She hated waiting for them to defog, looking like some kind of klutz. She didn't need help in that department when it came to her vision. Alyssa was one of those people who couldn't survive without her glasses or contacts.

That is, unless the world decided to orbit within an inch of her nose.

Further proving that point, no sooner had she walked into the lobby than she bumped shoulders with a man leaving.

"Sorry," she said quickly. He was too far away without her glasses on to be able to make out his face. But the blur responded all the same.

"It's okay," he said, before moving to the doors.

Alyssa smiled in his general direction and continued on to the closest teller line. By the time she was called up to a woman she knew as Missy Grayson, her glasses were clear again and had been replaced atop her nose. Now it was time for business.

"Deposit for Jeffries?" Missy guessed, already pulling up the account on the computer. That was a perk of living in a small town. Routines were noticed and information became common knowledge. Everyone knew Alyssa made the deposits.

"Yes, ma'am," Alyssa chirped, trying to match Missy's pep. "Then I think I'll take lunch at home so I can grab a warm pair of clothes and the umbrella I didn't think to take this morning."

Missy's face pinched.

"You know, I watched the news this morning and Carl didn't say anything about a storm coming at us," she said, nearing a full-out scolding for their local weatherman, despite the fact that he was not in the bank. "I told my husband he should even take the Jeep out with him to fish this morning. It has a soft top that's been off on account of it being summer, so I know he had one heck of a time with that. I bet I'm not going to hear the end of that any time soon."

"Hopefully he won't be too grumpy about it," Alyssa said. "When in doubt, blame the weatherman."

"You bet I am!"

The two laughed and started in on the technical parts of making a deposit. Alyssa was already imagining running back to her car and pointing it toward home. She had some leftovers from her night out with her friend Natalie on Saturday and could warm those up while she changed clothes. Her umbrella, though... Where was it? In the garage? When was the last time she'd seen—

A scream shattered her thoughts. Alyssa whirled around and found the source coming from a woman perhaps a few years younger than her twenty-seven. Aside from the scream, she was obviously distressed. Her expression was one of pure terror. It simultaneously confused Alyssa and put her on edge. It wasn't until the woman pointed toward the front doors that Alyssa understood.

And felt the same fear.

Two men and a woman, dripping wet, had come inside, the storm their backdrop. They wore matching gray jumpsuits, workmen's boots and, with her stomach plummeting to the floor, Alyssa realized, ski masks. Only their narrowed eyes and lips could be seen. Their hands were gloved too. Which made the fact that they were holding guns even more menacing.

"Anyone move and we'll start shooting," yelled the bigger man. He stood taller than his partners and looked like he had muscles beneath his getup. He was quick to move his gun and point it at the woman who had screamed. "Keep yelling like that and you'll be the first."

The young woman had backed up to one of the two desks on either side of the large open room. Ted Danfield, a loan officer in his fifties, had been standing in front of his desk talking to an elderly man. Now he reached out and grabbed the young woman's shoulders, pulling her the rest of the distance to his side. Her scream downgraded to a whimper.

"Don't you even think about it!"

Alyssa's attention moved to the female in the ski mask. She had stepped to the side and had her gun pointed at Robbie Rickman. Alyssa's stomach fell even more. He was the bank's lone security guard. Robbie had worked at the bank for years. Everyone who stepped through its front doors knew and loved him. He was kind, compassionate, and fiercely loved his wife of thirty years and three grown children.

So when the woman shot him, the ten or so patrons and employees of the bank collectively gasped. Alyssa went cold as Robbie dropped back on the floor. The gun he'd had in his hand hit the floor. Alyssa realized he'd been shot in the chest.

The woman quickly scooped up the gun and handed it back to the shorter of her partners. She kept her own gun held high. Her eyes skittered among them. Alyssa hoped the gunshot had been heard by the tenants next door, but as another loud crash of thunder sounded, preceded and followed by the hard rain, she doubted they knew the difference.

"Now that you know we're serious," said the bigger man, "let's get this moving along."

The two men shouted out orders left and right, swinging guns this way and that to help emphasize their urgency, while the woman stood silent, watching their every move. When they ordered everyone to the middle of the room, Alyssa had a hard time complying, thanks to fear that seemed to be trying to grow roots into the tile floor. But soon everyone except the other teller and the bank manager who had been taken to the back with the gunwoman were sitting in the middle of the room.

"Now," the bigger man started, walking to an elderly man and taking off his ball cap. He flipped it upside down. "Everyone put your cell phones, wallets and jewelry in here! If you have a purse, throw it next to our friend here who got shot!"

He didn't waste time letting that information set in. Moving quickly, the men and women of the bank put their phones, wallets and jewelry in the hat while others threw their purses near Robbie. When he got to Alyssa and shook the hat, she decided to do something risky.

She lied.

"I left everything in the car," she explained, holding her hands out to show they were empty. "I didn't want anything to get wet."

The man was close enough to smell. His scent was a mixture of rain and smoke. But not from cigarettes. He smelled more like he'd been to a barbecue recently. Or standing too close to a fire pit. It was an odd thought that pushed its way into Alyssa's head when she really should have focused on how his eyes narrowed even farther.

"Yeah, righ—"

"She just swallowed her ring!"

Alyssa and the gunman in front of her turned to look at the other gunman by the door. He was pointing to someone behind them both. Alyssa turned back around just in time to hear Missy cough.

"Did you really just swallow your ring?" the bigger gunman roared. He swung his gun over to point at her.

"You're damn right I swallowed my ring," she yelled back, fire in her eyes. "That ring was my mama's and her mama's before then. So unless you plan to wait it out, it's staying with me."

Alyssa felt a flash of pride for the woman—Southern ladies take their heirlooms seriously—however, it was short-lived. The gunman struck out with the butt of his gun and hit Missy across the head so fast that she didn't even have time to yell. But Alyssa did.

She crawled over to the woman just as she fell back against the tile. Blood burst from her cheek.

"Did I say you could move?" the gunman yelled at Alyssa. She froze next to Missy, knees against the floor and hands in the air.

She didn't respond to him. Nothing she said would have made the situation better when he was so obviously itching for some violence. Just like his woman partner. Robbie bleeding a few feet from them on the floor was a good indication of that.

"Get the rest of their stuff," said his partner, a reminder that he'd forgotten his original task. The gunman sneered down at Alyssa, just long enough to have his dark eyes imprinted in her memory for the rest of her life—whether or not she wanted it—and moved on to the last two people in their group.

Alyssa dropped her hands and felt her adrenaline spike. Moving so her back was to the gunman near the door, she reached out and helped Missy sit up. The woman's fire moments before had been doused. She was in pain. But she was going to have to forget that for a moment.

"Are you okay?" Alyssa whispered. With one hand she touched the open gash on her cheek and with the other she grabbed one of Missy's hands. "It'll be okay," she said before Missy could answer her question. The woman looked confused as Alyssa pulled her hand to her lap. From anyone else's point of view, Alyssa hoped it looked like she was just trying to console the woman.

When in reality she just wanted the woman to feel her cell phone, tucked out of sight in the raised waist of her skirt.

"Now, everyone keep their mouths shut! You make a move, you die," yelled the taller gunman. He took the hat full of their goods and gave it to the other gunman. They whispered a moment before the bigger man went to the back.

The bank patrons and employees were alone with the man who, Alyssa guessed, was the most observant of the three. She wasn't going to be able to use her phone while he was there. This realization inspired another risk on her part. One Alyssa hoped wouldn't get her or anyone else killed.

Still holding Missy's hand, she slipped her fingers into her skirt and pulled out her cell phone. Missy, bless her, didn't flinch as Alyssa put the phone against her palm. When she felt the woman's grip tighten around it, Alyssa put her hand back in Missy's lap and patted it twice.

Then Alyssa turned, heartbeat hammering in her chest.

"Can I go over to him?" Alyssa asked, nodding over to Robbie. "Someone needs to put pressure on his wound to try to stop the bleeding."

The man seemed, thankfully, less angry than his partners. Still, he was resistant. "I don't think so. You stay right there."

"But look at all that blood," she tried again, her voice near breaking. "Please, all I'm going to do is put my hands on it. Nothing else. *Please*."

The man cast a quick look at the group as a whole and then adjusted his gun's aim to the young woman in front. She flinched back into Ted's arms. The gunman looked at Alyssa.

"If you try anything, and I mean *anything*, I'll shoot her in the face. Got it?"

Alyssa nodded, amending her idea that this man was any less violent than his friends. She got up slowly, giving Missy time to hide the cell phone, hopefully, and walked with her hands held high over to Robbie's prone body.

She hadn't been lying. There *was* a lot of blood.

Since she had never been a part of the medical field in her life, she had no idea if putting pressure on a gunshot wound even worked. All she had to go by was TV shows and movies she'd seen. Still, she did as she said and dropped to the guard's side. Alyssa put one hand and then the other on top of the wound and pressed down. Warm blood squeezed out between her fingers. Robbie was still breathing, although the breaths were shallow.

The sound of rain and thunder continued in chorus for several minutes. Alyssa kept her eyes off Missy, since the gunman seemed to be looking in her direction every few seconds, but she prayed the woman had made the call to the cops. After another few minutes, Alyssa came to the conclusion that she hadn't.

But then Alyssa spied movement on the other side of the glass doors and several things happened all at once.

The gunman had started to turn toward the doors when she found herself speaking up again.

"He really needs a doctor soon," she said, drawing his attention toward her.

He opened his mouth to talk just as his partners came back into the lobby.

"Cops," the woman yelled.

The gunman at the door didn't hesitate. He whirled around.

Then the gunfire and screaming started.

All Alyssa had time to do was throw herself over Robbie and hope she'd live long enough to tell her sister that, for once, she'd had her cell phone right when she needed it.

Chapter Two

Caleb Foster cursed something awful.

"How do you even function out here in this?"

Deputy Dante Mills let out a laugh.

"You get used to it," he said. "Just one of those things."

Caleb, a man who'd spent the majority of his career—and life—in Portland, Oregon, might have been okay with the blanket heat that the small town of Carpenter, Alabama, was throwing at him, but its humidity was another problem altogether.

It was one thing to be stuck in the heat. It was another to feel like you were drowning in it.

"I don't want to get used to this," he said sourly. He didn't care if Dante heard him. Ever since his transfer to the Riker County Sheriff's Department had been approved one month ago, he hadn't been making it a secret he was unhappy. Not that he'd had much of an alternative option, though. "I want some air that doesn't make me feel like I'm swimming standing up."

Dante chuckled. "You city boys sure do complain a lot."

Caleb was about to ask what his partner's definition of "city boy" was when they came to a stop in the
parking lot. He decided he'd ask that question later.
Right now he was concerned about why the sheriff
had called him in minutes after their shift started. He
might not have wanted the Alabama weather, but he
did want his job.

The Riker County Sheriff's Department stood between the local television station and the county courthouse, all three in the very heart of the town. With
two stories and faded brick and concrete, the department faced one of Carpenter's main streets and was
subsequently always busy. This was a familiar sight
for Caleb, and while he wouldn't admit it to any of
the other deputies, the busyness made him a little less
homesick.

He followed Dante through the front doors and into
the lobby. A pretty blonde dispatcher named Cassie,
who was rumored to be as tough as nails when needed,
was in the center of the room talking to another woman.
Both had cups of coffee in their hands.

"Hey, guys," she greeted, cheer clear in her tone.
"Happy Monday!"

"There's no such thing as happy Mondays, Cassie,"
Dante pointed out, though he smiled as he made the
little quip. It seemed the whole of the department func-
tioned like that. One person saying something, only
for another to add on something equally clever or nice.
Most of the time it was inside jokes or references beyond Caleb's knowledge. He tried not to let it bother
him. He was the new guy, after all. Plus, once he was

done with his time in Riker County, he'd go back home. So what if he wasn't in sync with his colleagues now? He hoped it wouldn't matter in a few months or, God forbid, a year.

"I'm going to go see the sheriff," Caleb said, nodding to the two women. "I'll catch you after."

"Good luck," Dante called after him.

Caleb hoped he didn't need it.

He walked out of the lobby and down the hallway where the offices were located. The sheriff's was smack in the middle, nameplate auspiciously brighter than the others. Caleb slowed, stilling himself. He knew he was more on the pricklier side of a good personality. Quiet too. So far he hadn't met anyone in the department with the same disposition. Again, he didn't mind if the rest of them didn't like him. However, he did want the sheriff to find him at least agreeable. He tried on a smile that felt forced before knocking on the doorframe of the open door.

"Come in."

The muscles in Caleb's smile tightened as soon as he saw the man hunched over his desk.

Billy Reed by no means should have been an intimidating man. From first glance he was too tall, too lean, and had dark hair that was too long. Maybe that was just Caleb's opinion bleeding through, though, considering he was the opposite of the sheriff.

At five-eleven, Caleb was a man who believed in the gym as much as he believed that anyone with a clipboard on the sidewalk ready to talk about political candidates or a chance to win a cruise was supposed to be ignored. With his solid shoulders, trim body and a hard jaw, the only thing that looked remotely playful about him—according to his sister—was his golden hair, cut close but still with enough curl to annoy him. He sported a goatee but had been playing with the idea of shaving it since he'd come to town, as it was just another thing that made him hot in an already hot-as-hell town. Luckily, he still looked his age of thirty without it. He knew the sheriff was on the young side too—especially for his position—but Caleb couldn't read the man to guess an accurate age. Billy Reed was a mystery, while Caleb was the kind of man who looked like "what you see is what you get."

It was apparent that everyone in the department not only respected the sheriff, but liked him. And just as quickly when the man gave an order, it didn't matter if anyone was his friend or not. Everyone listened without skipping a beat.

So when he told Caleb to take a seat, Caleb took the seat without arguing.

"I'm going to cut right to the chase," Reed started. He threaded his hands on top of the desk. "I'm pulling you off patrol and putting you at the courthouse."

Caleb opened his mouth, ready to complain—respect and authority for the sheriff be damned—but Reed stopped him. He held his hand up for silence. "When Chief Thomas called me and asked if I had a spot for you, I was skeptical. But I've known Thomas a long time and he's a good judge of character, so I looked past what happened and gave you a chance. But while you've done a good job so far, being new has its own set of demands." He thrust his thumb over his shoulder to point back at the wall behind him. "That includes pulling courtroom deputy when I need you to."

Again, before Caleb could protest, the sheriff handed him a newspaper. A picture of a storefront with caution tape across it took up a spot above the fold.

"Almost a year ago to the day, three armed suspects used a storm as a cover to try to rob a bank a few miles from here," he started. "There were nine hostages, including bank employees and a security guard who was shot when they entered. A woman inside was able to get a call out to us, but when we arrived the suspects opened fire. In total, three people were killed, including one of the gunmen."

Caleb could tell by the way the sheriff's expression turned to pain that the other two deaths had hurt. In a small town like Carpenter, he'd probably known the victims personally. Something Caleb was in no way used to. When he was a cop in Portland, he'd dealt with mostly strangers. Their indiscretions hadn't affected him outside of his having to deal with them as his job.

The sheriff seemed to collect himself. He pointed to the newspaper again.

"The trial takes place next week and it's going to draw a lot of attention," he continued. "I'm adding you as backup, along with the current court deputy, Stanley King."

"Wait, so I'm not even *lead* court deputy?" Caleb had to interject. It was bad enough he'd lost his reputation and his position in Portland. Never mind he had to be transferred to keep from being completely jobless. But now he was expected to go to the bottom of the totem pole to not even being *on* the totem pole?

Sheriff Reed didn't bat an eyelid.

"I'll be out of town during the beginning of the trial, as well as Chief Deputy Simmons and lead detective Matt Walker, or else I would be over there too. But as it stands, I'm looking to you," Reed said. "This may not be your dream job, but it's what you have and you can either complain about it or impress me. After what happened in Portland, any good marks on your résumé will help."

Caleb wanted to argue but knew he couldn't.

The sheriff seemed to realize he'd made a good point. He grinned. "And, hey, look on the bright side. Air-conditioning!"

ALYSSA WAS ANGRY. She was nervous too, but mostly angry.

Standing outside the county courthouse, she was dressed in her best and ready to finally testify against what locals had dubbed the "Storm Chasers."

After the gunfire died down a year ago, she'd thought the terror was over. She'd focused on moving past that day and trying for a happier existence because of it. But then the nightmares had started. In them she'd seen the dark eyes of Dupree Slater, the taller gunman, hungry for violence, peering down at her. No regard for life. Especially not hers. Thinking of him and his only living partner left, Anna Kim, she still felt a flood of fear beating against her mental dam of calm. That dam didn't always hold, despite the fact that both Dupree and Anna had been in custody for a year, but today she needed it to keep its place.

She shook her head, trying to physically get rid of the way Dupree's dark eyes seemed to try to eat her whole.

But then, just as quickly, thinking of him led to the image of his partner, a man named Kevin Bates, lying dead on the floor a few feet from her. Farther away one of the bank tellers, Larissa Colt, and a local patron, Carl Redford, lying in their own pools of blood. Gunned down before the deputies could save them. They'd all been so afraid. The fear lingered to this day.

And just like that, Alyssa's familiar fear was replaced with anger.

Alyssa hadn't known Larissa well and she hadn't met Carl officially, but she knew that they had been good people. Their deaths had been senseless and cruel. Both had rocked the community.

Alyssa took a deep breath and righted the purse on her shoulder. She was here for them, for herself and for Carpenter as a whole. Justice needed to be had. And it was now or never.

She walked through the double doors into the courthouse, knowing she was early but ready to get it over with. Her mind was tearing through a hundred different thoughts, trying to find a happy one to stave off her growing anxiety. So much so that she lost focus on what was right in front of her.

"Hey," a man said. The voice was deep and even and snapped her out of her own thoughts. She turned her attention to a man standing next to the set of metal detectors that visitors had to pass through to get into the courtroom. Alyssa did a double take.

His Riker County Sheriff's Department uniform and the belt lined with cuffs and a holster for his service weapon gave him away as a courtroom deputy. However, his job designation wasn't what made her mentally hiccup.

The first word that clawed itself out of her mind was *hot*. It was such a quick, unexpected thought that heat began to crawl up her neck.

With a tan complexion that reminded her of caramel, green eyes rimmed with gold, golden hair that looked ripe for twisting with her finger and a jaw that had been chiseled straight from a statue, the deputy wasn't what she'd expected to see in the courthouse. Or in Carpenter. Let alone addressing her directly.

"Excuse me?" she said lamely, hoping he hadn't somehow heard her thoughts.

In turn the deputy didn't seem to be distracted by her looks, to her slight disappointment, but was motioning to her purse with no real enthusiasm. She looked down at it, confused, until he explained.

"I need to look inside it before you can go into the courtroom."

The heat crawling up her neck made its way into her cheeks. She was half-certain she could boil water if you put a pot of it against her skin. It had been a long time since she'd blushed with such intensity, as if she were some schoolgirl.

"Oh yeah, sorry about that." She handed him the

purse, fumbling a little in the middle, and watched as he opened and inspected the inside of it.

Alyssa averted her eyes to the doors a few feet from her. The deputy might have been unexpectedly attractive, but one look at those doors and that novelty was being replaced with nerves again.

"Are there a lot of people in there yet?" she asked the lone deputy.

He looked up from her purse, seemingly okay with it, and passed it back to her. He nodded. "More than I thought would show up this early. But I think a lot of them just came for the show."

There was distaste in his words and she agreed with it. Small towns equaled big reactions to anomalous events. Good, bad or otherwise. Plus, somehow the robbery felt intimate to her. An experience no one understood unless it had happened to them. She could understand the loved ones of those who had been inside the bank, but for the people who showed up for the basic need for gossip, she held no love.

Alyssa took her purse back and inhaled a big breath. She started to walk forward but found her feet hesitating.

"Dupree Slater isn't in there yet, right?" she asked just to make sure. The deputy's golden brows drew in together. "He was one of the gunmen."

The man who survived, she wanted to add.

"No. He won't be escorted in until the beginning of the trial."

Alyssa exhaled. At least she had a few more minutes to collect herself before she saw her own personal nightmare in person again.

"Are you a family or friend of his?" the deputy asked. "Of Slater's?"

Alyssa felt her face draw in, eyes narrowing into angry slits, before the heat of anger began to burn beneath her breast. Without giving her mind permission, she thought again of what had happened in the bank. Like a movie scene left on repeat. The spot on her back began to burn in unison with fresh anger, as if it had been lit on fire and she was forced to bear the flames.

No, she didn't want to be associated with Dupree Slater ever. Not as his friend. Not as his family. And most certainly not as his victim. That thought alone put a little more bite into her response than she'd meant.

"I am *not* a part of his family and certainly not his friend," she almost hissed. "I'm here to testify against him."

She didn't wait for the deputy to respond. In fact, she didn't even look for his reaction. Instead she pitched her head up high and marched into the courtroom. Ready to get the Storm Chasers and the damage they'd done out of her life. She wanted to move on and leave that nightmare behind.

No.

She *needed* to.

Chapter Three

Caleb was perplexed. Not a word he often thought about but one that fit the bill as he watched the courtroom doors shut behind the woman. He'd been at the courthouse since it opened, and she had been, by far, the most interesting part of his Monday. And he doubted she even meant to be interesting.

The analytical side of his brain, the skills in reading body language and social interactions that he liked to think he'd honed through his career, had locked on to her expression, trying to read her. To figure her out.

She had run a gauntlet of emotions across her face in the span of less than a minute. Fear, concern, anger, defiance and something he hadn't been able to pin down. A mystery element that snagged his attention. Then, as quickly as she'd shown up, she was gone. In her wake a taste of vulnerability that had intrigued him even more.

Who was she?

And why did he want to know?

"Was that Alyssa?"

Caleb spun around. He was surprised to see an older man dressed in a suit standing so close. Caleb hadn't heard him walk up. Leave it to a beautiful woman to break his focus so quickly. Though, if he was being honest, that hadn't happened in a long time.

It was Caleb's turn to say "Excuse me?"

The man pointed to the doors. "The woman you were just talking to, was it Alyssa Garner?"

"I didn't catch a name," Caleb admitted.

"Oh, I thought you two knew each other. I saw you talking when I walked in."

Caleb wondered why the man cared but still explained. "I asked if she was a family or friend of Slater's, one of the gunmen from the robbery."

It was like something was in the water in Carpenter, Alabama. As soon as the name left Caleb's mouth, the man's expression darkened. Unlike the woman, the man stayed on that emotion. If his skin had been lighter, Caleb would bet it would have been red from it. That was what rage did. Turned you raw. Caleb knew what that looked like—felt like too—and the man was suddenly waist-deep in it.

"You know, she had the same reaction," Caleb had to point out. Again the cop side of his brain was piqued. He wished he'd done more research into the robbery other than reading the newspaper article the sheriff had given him. Then again, it wasn't a necessity for him to research a case he wasn't a part of. Especially since he'd get a recap from the future proceedings.

"You'll find no love for that man in this town. Not after what they did. Not after what *he* did." The man touched a spot on his chest. "You know, his partner, Anna Kim, shot me, and I still hate Dupree more."

Caleb couldn't stop his eyebrow from rising.

"You must be new to town," the man guessed.

Caleb nodded and was given the man's hand in return.

"I'm Robbie," he said. "I was the security guard. A good lot of luck that did anybody. Less than a few seconds after they came in, I was down for the count. After I was shot they let me just lie there in my own blood, ignoring me as if I was some character in a video game or whatnot. They didn't care if I lived or died. And I would've died had Alyssa there not been as crafty as she was." He pointed at the courtroom doors.

"Crafty?"

"She hid her cell phone until one of the tellers could call 911 and then distracted the gunman on watch by coming to my aid."

Robbie put his hand on his chest again and pushed.

"She kept me from bleeding out and got a front row view when the shooting started. She watched that… that *man* kill two people—two *good* people—in cold blood."

"The paper said they died in the cross fire," Caleb remembered.

Robbie looked disgusted.

"I don't believe that for a second," he said. "Dupree Slater is an evil sumbitch. Pure and simple. He wanted to kill us all and probably regrets he couldn't get the job done."

Caleb didn't know what to say. In his career he'd seen what he thought of as pure evil. Slater, although Caleb knew he was in no way a good man, didn't seem to fit his definition of it. He'd just been a man who'd robbed a bank and gotten in a shoot-out with the cops. He'd been a piss-poor shot and people had died because of it. If anything, his female partner had seemed like the worst of the two. It was common knowledge that the first thing she'd done was shoot the security guard in the chest, which apparently was the man standing in front of Caleb.

Maybe Robbie sensed Caleb's thoughts.

"Not convinced he's evil? You want to know something that they didn't put in the paper? Something that was kept out to try to protect her privacy?" Robbie lowered his voice. A group of people could be seen milling outside the front glass double doors. The residents of Carpenter were downright punctual. Robbie waited until Caleb turned his gaze back to him. When he spoke, there was no denying his anger again. His rage. "When the shooting started, Alyssa Garner threw herself over me—someone who could have been dead any moment—to protect me. She could have run and tried to hide like the others, but no, she covered me up like she was indebted to me. Like I was a good friend or even family. And by some miracle she wasn't hit in the process. But you want to know what happened after they surrendered?"

Caleb might not have known the woman named Alyssa past a minute ago, but he knew he wasn't going to like the answer already.

Robbie nearly bit the words out. "Before anyone could stop him, Dupree Slater walked over to us and shot Alyssa right in the back." He let that sink in. "Now, you tell me. What kind of man does that? What kind of man shoots an unarmed young woman who was just trying to save an old man like me *in the back*?"

"Not a good one," Caleb answered. He was surprised at the anger growing in him. It wasn't a good feeling. Not after what had happened back in Portland. He tried to distance himself from it, but then he pictured the woman who had stood before him only a few minutes beforehand.

Her light auburn hair had been pulled back, showing blue eyes, bright and clear and nice. They'd sized him up and then left him alone, traveling back to see what must have been the memory of Dupree Slater killing people before he'd tried to kill her too. He hadn't been able to see if her smile lit up the rest of her expression. Dupree had stripped her of it simply by her recalling a memory.

Caleb now felt like he needed to apologize to her, which was absurd. He hadn't known her name or what had happened when he asked about the bank robber.

Robbie, seemingly coming down off his emotional high, let out a long exhale. It dragged his body down. His expression softened. He gave Caleb a tired smile.

"You seem like a man who's dealt with bad before," he said, reaching out to pat Caleb on the shoulder.

The contact surprised and unsettled him. Another sentiment he wasn't used to from the general public in Portland.

"But know that just because we're a small community, it doesn't mean we're all good here either. There's

bad everywhere. Even in a small place like Carpenter."
The man gave another weak smile and then was gone.

Caleb went back to his job. He decided it best to
keep his mouth shut as he manned the detector. Instead he tried to catalog everyone who walked into
the courtroom with a new perspective. Now he felt a
small connection to a case he hadn't even bothered to
research. It was irrational to feel involved, or, as his
sister would say, maybe it was compassion attaching
his thoughts to the woman named Alyssa. He'd never
met her before and doubted he'd have a chance to talk
to her ever again, but still he felt anger for what had
happened to her. That feeling made him question every
person who filed into the courtroom and his or her part
in the robbery.

So when a man dressed in a suit wearing a pair of
horn-rimmed glasses walked toward him and stopped
just shy of the metal detector, Caleb was already trying to figure him out.

How did he fit into that day?

Had he been one of the hostages?

Had he known someone on the inside?

Or was he just there to gawk?

"Has it started yet?" the man asked, motioning to
the closed doors.

Caleb shook his head. "Not yet."

The man started to turn away.

"You aren't going in?" Caleb asked after him, surprised.

"No, I'm only here to wait for a friend," he said.
"I'll do that outside."

The man smiled, adjusted his glasses and was out the front doors in a flash.

Caleb would later pinpoint that smile as the moment he knew something bad was about to happen. But in the present he would try to pretend everything was all right, dismissing the feeling in lieu of doing his job correctly. He'd already almost lost his career because he'd let himself get carried away once. Plus, like he'd told Robbie, he *was* new in town. That man, and his out-of-place smile, could have been one of the nicest locals he'd ever meet. Who was *he* to judge? Especially after what he'd done?

So he'd let his mind swim back to dry land and stood diligently at his post. This was just another job he had to do—and do well—to get back to where he should be. Back in Portland, away from small towns and their problems. Away from everyone knowing your name. Away from the humidity, droves of mosquitoes and copious amounts of sweet tea. He didn't have time for distractions. He needed to focus on the end goal.

But then no sooner had he gotten the thought than the fire alarms started going off.

THE JUDGE WASN'T even in the room before Alyssa and the rest of the courtroom were being ushered outside.

Just when I was getting up my nerve, she thought in the middle of the group. Together they all created a blob of people talking loudly to one another, to the point where even her thoughts became muddled. She tried to look for someone in charge to ask them if it was a false alarm or if the fire was real but couldn't see anyone other than her courtroom companions. At least there was a smiling one among them, looking right at her.

Robbie picked his way through the crowd to stop in front of her.

"It's always something, isn't it?" he greeted, motioning back to the building. The sirens screeched something awful. While Alyssa had been itching to get everything done with, she was at least thankful to be out of that noise. The beginnings of a tension headache were starting to swarm in the back of her head.

She snorted.

"We spent a year waiting for this day," she said. "What's a few more minutes?"

"Your optimism is always refreshing," he said, knowing full well she'd been sarcastic.

She smiled up at him.

In the last year, she'd grown close to Robbie and his wife, Eleanor. She'd made sure they both knew that they owed her nothing in trying to protect Robbie at the bank. Mostly because she hadn't done a thing to actually protect him. With or without her body covering his, he'd still almost died. But then they'd point out that if she hadn't been where she was, Dupree might not have shot her.

"Nowhere in that bank was safe as long as Dupree and Anna were inside," she had often countered.

They would quiet then, remembering Larissa and Carl had been shot too. And nowhere near where Robbie and Alyssa had been.

Still, Alyssa and the Rickmans had grown close through more than any sense of warranted or unwarranted life debt. Which made her feel more comfortable being candid around either of them. She lowered her voice and admitted something she wouldn't have said otherwise.

"I'm a little glad I get a break from seeing Dupree, though. Between the newspapers, the local news channels and the occasional nightmare, I'm tired of seeing him."

Robbie nodded.

"Even Eleanor can't stand to turn the TV on lately. But, like I tell her, this is our last hurdle and then we're done," he said. He reached over and patted her arm. "After this we can all move on and live happy, full lives with a completely rational fear of banks for the rest of those happy, full lives."

Alyssa gave him a smile for his attempt at humor and hoped that was true. Closure for her would be when the Storm Chasers landed behind bars for life, never to hurt her or anyone else ever again.

"Can I have everyone's attention?"

They turned to none other than Judge Anderson, the judge for this case. Her robes moved in the stiff breeze as she descended the entrance stairs and came to a stop in front of the crowd. Another courtroom deputy, an older man Alyssa recognized but couldn't recall his name, stood at her side. Alyssa wondered where the other man was. The golden-haired deputy with the muscled body in no way hiding beneath his uniform.

A little bit of heat started to swirl behind her cheeks at the thought of that muscled body. Why she never met men like him during the everyday routines of her life, she'd never know.

"I wanted to personally tell you all that we'll be taking a recess until this afternoon at one o'clock," she said, her voice carrying clear across the distance. "I am sorry for the inconvenience."

A series of groans erupted through the crowd, followed by the clash of everyone talking at once. Alyssa was one of them.

"Speaking of hurdles," she deadpanned.

Robbie let out a hoot of laughter.

"Why don't we turn that frown upside down and take my beautiful wife out for some coffee and cake?" he said with a pat on her back. "Because I know she probably needs some caffeine considering how late she's running anyways. My treat. What do you say?"

Alyssa felt her lips upturn in a smile.

"You had me at coffee," she said, nodding. "But isn't it a little too early for cake?"

Robbie laughed again. "According to my wife, there's never a wrong time for cake."

Chapter Four

Caleb was pacing. An action he actively tried to avoid doing.

For one, people who paced were *not* in control of their current situation. Hence the nervous movement edged with anxiety and uncertainty. His career—and his personality if he was being frank—had made his desire to be in control, well, desirable. So he wasn't a fan of walking back and forth trying to burn anxious energy. Second, pacing usually meant someone was waiting for *something* to happen, and patience was also not Caleb's strongest suit.

Yet here he was, moving back and forth just inside the entrance of the courthouse on repeat. Burning a hole in the lobby's faded carpet.

It had been three hours since the fire alarm went off. Since there was no fire in the building, or even smoke, Caleb had put his bet on the culprit being a punk kid or a disgruntled attendee. Someone who wanted to break up their day with a little excitement. That is, until he'd seen the alarm that had been pulled.

Smashed beyond recognition. Obliterated. It had

been a miracle the sirens had managed to keep blaring after the alarm had been pulled and then destroyed. They'd had to wait for the fire department to shut it all down. One firefighter had whistled low at the broken shell of the alarm and asked what was the point of pulling it *and* breaking it.

Caleb hadn't had an answer. He'd officially gone on alert, a feeling of foreboding lying heavy in the pit of his stomach. Hours later, that heaviness hadn't gone away. Not when deputies had come over from the sheriff's department next door. Not when they had gone through the entire building, room by room, looking for anything suspicious. And not when the security footage hadn't been helpful, thanks to a gap in the recording, which was due to poor funding.

"It happens sometimes," the other deputy had said with a shrug. "The courthouse isn't the only place in town waiting on funding to come through to get a better system."

"Sounds like an excuse," Caleb said beneath his breath. The deputy hadn't heard him, and he wanted to keep it that way.

Again, he didn't know how Carpenter, or Riker County, truly worked. He didn't know their struggles or their points of pride. Jumping to conclusions about a broken fire alarm at an underfunded courthouse wasn't something he needed to do. He certainly didn't need to overstep his job description by trying to investigate a situation that probably wasn't anything more than someone caught in the heat of the moment and deciding to break something.

At that thought, Caleb's body went cold.

His hands balled into fists.

His thoughts turned tumultuous in a fraction of a second. Memories of what he'd done flew through his head.

"Foster! Stop! Dammit, Foster! STOP!"

But Caleb hadn't stopped.

And now he was in Riker County because of it.

He began to pace again.

ALYSSA WAVED GOODBYE to Robbie and Eleanor. They drove away from the courthouse in Robbie's little red pickup, both smiling as they disappeared down the street. Alyssa couldn't help but smile too. There was nothing like spending a few hours at Danny's—a local café with the best cake, according to Eleanor—with the couple to get her back into a good mood. Them laughing and smiling at each other had been contagious. Being with them always reminded Alyssa she was missing something they had been lucky enough to find. A partner. A best friend. Someone who would buy her morning cake without flinching.

Being that close to such a strong couple brought out a sense of peace in her too. Like the sight of calm waters after looking over the edge of your boat.

It had helped that, despite it being the day of the trial, they had sidestepped any talk of the Storm Chasers. It was a groove that had become familiar with them

over the last year. A rhythm that had become second
nature. They talked about happier topics, even mun-
dane ones. Anything that filled the time.

But now Alyssa was back, staring at the front of
the courthouse.

How she wished she could go inside, tell the jury
what she'd seen and then watch as Dupree and Anna
were led away in cuffs. Forever.

Alyssa let out a long sigh. She still had a few hours
to go before she could get her wish.

"I might as well go soak in a bath," she muttered to
herself. If there was ever an answer to quell unwanted
anxiety, a quiet, citrus-scented bath had to be at the
top of the to-do list. She had started to walk around
the building, mind already made up, when the sound
of footsteps sounded behind her.

"Excuse me!"

Alyssa turned to see a man jogging toward her. He
was brandishing a set of keys.

"You dropped these," he explained, motioning to
where she'd been standing when she was dropped off.

"Really?" Even though they were clearly hers—the
wineglass pendant Gabby had given her was glinting
in the sunlight—Alyssa still opened her purse to look
inside and confirm they weren't there. "Wow. I don't
know how I did that. I could've sworn they were buried in my purse."

The man pushed his glasses up his nose. Alyssa
mimicked the motion on reflex. Gabby always made
fun of her for the "nerd" move, but when Alyssa was

around her own glasses-wearing kind, she was happy for the little inclusion.

"You must have been thinking of other things," he offered. "This Storm Chasers business has a lot of people around here distracted."

Alyssa took her keys and tried on a polite smile. Though she didn't like the way the man had said "here," she agreed with him.

"Yes, it definitely has the attention of the entire community. It'll be nice when it's all over." She jingled her keys, wanting to end the conversation. "Thank you for being less distracted than me."

The man grinned.

"No problem," he said. "Have a nice day."

The way he said the last part, just like the word *here*, was so odd that it caught Alyssa a little off guard. She hesitated a few seconds too long. His smile wavered.

"Thanks again." She tried to recover, heat exploding into her cheeks. She turned away and hurried to her car. When had she dropped her keys? And how?

She tried to mentally retrace her actions, and none of them included her opening her purse, let alone taking her keys out.

"Maybe I *am* way more stressed than I originally thought," she mumbled, unlocking her door with the key fob. The day was hot and twinged with growing humidity. She held the unlock button down a few seconds longer. The front windows rolled down in response. She waited a moment, still trying to puzzle out the question of her keys leaving her possession, as a wave of heat poured out. It pressed against her skin with a maliciousness she'd come to expect from Alabama summers.

And here she was, about to go get into a hot bath. She sighed, wondering how that made sense, and tossed her purse into the passenger's seat. She smoothed down the back of her pencil skirt and plopped down into the driver's seat.

Click.

Alyssa paused, confused.

Click.

"What?" she muttered, trying to find the source of the noise. Last time she checked, her car had never *clicked* before. "I swear if it's the AC crapping out…"

Alyssa didn't have to look far. "Oh my God."

CALEB'S PACING GAVE him a front row view of the woman named Alyssa Garner. He watched as Robbie and, presumably, his wife had dropped her off and then watched as she had started for the parking lot.

For a moment she had seemed happy, lighter than she had been that morning. Almost carefree. Her head was tilted up, lips in the same direction, and her shoulders were relaxed. At some point, wherever she'd gone, she'd even let her hair down. It cascaded over her shoulders and back, shining in the sun, more red than brown as it had looked inside. He wondered how she looked without her trendy black pair of frames on. Either way, he couldn't deny that he found her attractive.

Alyssa seemed to be a quiet woman with an equally quiet beauty.

But Caleb now wondered if that was true…especially after what she'd done at the bank.

That anger that had startled him before began to rise in his chest again just thinking about the man Dupree Slater.

Caleb wondered if she had a scar from him.

Surprised again, he caught his thoughts before they became even darker.

He didn't know Alyssa. At least not personally. He hadn't even known she existed until that morning. He wasn't close to her or, in fact, to anyone in Carpenter or Riker County. Having feelings for her like he was didn't make sense. And wasn't wanted.

You won't be here long, he thought, resolute. *Keep your head down, follow orders, and then you're back home.*

Caleb had started to turn away from the glass doors, giving Alyssa some privacy and his thoughts a firm shake away from her, when movement stilled his motion. A man ran up to her. He gave Alyssa something, but from Caleb's angle he couldn't see what it was. Or what the man looked like.

Could be a friend, he reasoned. *Or a boyfriend.*

No sooner had he thought that than he dismissed it. While he couldn't see the man's expression, he watched as Alyssa's changed. Her brow furrowed and she frowned. Then she was smiling, but in a flash that smile fell away.

She was confused or unhappy. He couldn't tell which, but it was enough to keep him watching as she left the man's side and went to her car.

The man watched her go. He must have known her, Caleb thought. Why else would he just stand there watching?

Maybe he was admiring her too?

Either way, Caleb didn't like it.

He left his post and stepped out into the heat. The humidity was suffocating. It amazed him that it still caught him off guard. And that people chose to live in it.

"Excuse me?" Caleb called out.

The man didn't move.

Caleb's gut started to talk.

And he didn't like what it was trying to say.

"Hey," he tried again, taking a few steps forward and giving the man the benefit of the doubt. Maybe he hadn't heard him. "Hey, buddy!"

The man, now a few yards away, turned around. It was a slow, lazy movement. He didn't seem surprised at a slightly agitated court deputy's appearance, but the same couldn't be said for Caleb.

"You."

The man with the horn-rimmed glasses grinned. "Hello, Deputy. How can I help you?"

Caleb hung back at the bottom of the stairs. His gut was full-out yelling now. It prompted him to *really* look at the man.

Over six feet and thin, the man wore glasses, but

they had the opposite effect that Alyssa's had on her. Instead of giving the impression that he might be on the quiet side, they turned his sharp facial features and thinness into an overall look of aggression. The descriptor popped into Caleb's head so fast he realized he'd already had the thought the first time he saw the man. It didn't help that his body was seemingly speaking an entirely different language with how he was dressed—slacks, a dark red vest and dress shoes—and where he was.

He was comfortable *and* anxious. While he greeted Caleb with a grin, Caleb noticed one of his hands against his thighs, his fingers tapping out a rhythm. A nervous tic. An anxious activity like pacing but more controlled.

"What are you doing out here?" Caleb asked, acutely aware of the space between them. "Are you still waiting for your friend?"

The man's grin widened.

"You're good with faces," he said. "I didn't think you'd remember mine. But no, I've already seen my friend." He glanced toward the parking lot and then back to Caleb. "I'm on my way now. Have a good day, Deputy."

He didn't wait for a response. Putting both hands in his pockets, he moved away from Caleb to the sidewalk in front of the courthouse. Caleb thought about following him and demanding his name at the very least, but then his gut was twisting again.

He turned back to the parking lot.

Something felt off.

Alyssa's outline could be seen in her car in the middle of the visitors' lot, but she hadn't started it yet. Why she hadn't at least turned the ignition just to get the AC going, Caleb didn't know. Maybe Alabamians were made with more heat resistance than he was.

Still, the lot wasn't in the shade and the sun wasn't being kind. It beat down on the little Honda like it had been doing all morning.

The inside had to be hot as hell.

Caleb took a moment to debate whether or not he should check on her. Maybe she was having issues with her car. Or maybe the man with the glasses had said something that upset her. Maybe it wasn't any of his business either way.

Caleb adjusted his belt and turned back toward the courthouse.

Keep your head low, he reminded himself. *It isn't your place.*

Halfway up the stairs, his feet stalled.

No, it was going to be impossible to keep his head low when his gut was telling him to do otherwise.

It was *so* hot.

Alyssa's muscles were straining to not move while sweat began to roll down her skin without any such constraints. While the windows were down, no breeze moved throughout the car. Her only company was a stifling, unforgiving blanket of wet heat. It was turning her situation into more of a nightmare. The hammering of her heart hadn't broken the silence, but that didn't mean it wasn't beating against her chest in terror.

Sure, there was a chance she was overreacting. *Paranoia*. But what if she wasn't?

She tried to take in another deep breath to help tamp down her nerves.

It didn't help.

Especially not when someone approached the open window.

"Excuse me?"

Alyssa let out a shriek and gave a small jump in her seat. It was enough movement to make her adrenaline surge higher.

"Sorry, I didn't mean to startle you," the man said.

Alyssa allowed herself just enough movement to look at the stranger. Although he wasn't just any man. The golden-haired deputy was staring back at her. She found his eyes, the perfect middle ground between golden and green, and felt genuine relief at his presence. However, she guessed her expression said something else entirely. His light brows drew together so quickly that she knew *he* knew something was wrong. "Are you okay?" he asked, voice ringing with authority.

Alyssa took a deep, wavering breath. "Have you seen the *Lethal Weapon* movies? You know, with Mel Gibson and Danny Glover as cops?" she asked.

The deputy raised an eyebrow but nodded. "Yeah…"

"Well, you know the one where Danny Glover's character is sitting on the toilet?"

"Yeah, that's the second movie," he said. "When he realizes there's a bomb strapped to it. Why?"

A chill ran up Alyssa's spine at that four-letter word.

"Well, this is probably going to sound ridiculous," she started, "but I think there's a bomb under my seat."

Chapter Five

The deputy squatted down on the other side of the door so that his gaze was level with hers. Under any other circumstances she probably would have been distracted by the proximity, but right now her mind kept going to what might or might not be beneath her seat.

"You're going to have to elaborate on that one for me."

Alyssa licked her lips. They were already drying out despite her lipstick.

"Okay, so when I sat down I heard something click," she started. "I hadn't turned the car on yet, so it confused me. Then I heard two more clicks and actually *felt* those coming from under me. Under my seat. And then I saw the light."

"The light?"

Alyssa moved her head to try to motion to the floorboard. She still wasn't about to move the rest of her body if she could help it. Her hands were on her lap, fused together with sweat and nerves. In the movie, once Danny Glover's character had gotten off the toilet it had exploded. And she was *not* about to blow up in a Honda.

"I can see the reflection of a red light blinking on the floorboard," she answered. "It's faint but it's there. And it hasn't stopped blinking."

The deputy didn't ask for permission, not that she was going to begrudge him for the invasion anyway, and moved his head in through the window to look toward her feet. Alyssa caught a whiff of either shampoo or body wash that smelled intoxicating as he moved into her personal space. Some kind of musk and spice infusion. Something she definitely shouldn't be distracted by at the moment.

"I know I could be overreacting, but I guess I've just seen so many movies and TV shows where clicks and flashing lights equals bombs," she admitted. The fear that had tensed her every muscle was now starting to feel a little silly. "And if it isn't a bomb, which it *probably* isn't, I'll just be mortified for life."

The man pulled out of the space and back into a squat next to the door. His expression gave nothing away.

"Can I open your door?" he asked, voice even.

Silly thought or not, the request scared Alyssa.

"If there's a bomb under your seat, opening the door shouldn't trigger it," he added.

"But if it does?" she couldn't help asking. A drop of sweat rolled down the side of her face. It was *so* hot.

The deputy's expression stayed neutral when he answered.

"Then, I promise you, we won't know the difference."

Alyssa felt her eyes widen.

"I don't know if I'm happy with that logic."

The man didn't apologize for it.

"I won't do it if you don't want me to," he said. "I just need to take a closer look."

Alyssa chewed on her lip but nodded.

"What's your name?" she tacked on. The man raised his eyebrow. "Just in case we do blow up."

"Caleb Foster."

"I'm Alyssa Garner," she introduced. "I would shake your hand, but I'm terrified that if I move I'll— Well, you know…"

Caleb flashed a smile. It didn't last long.

"Then let me do the moving for now," he said. Alyssa watched as his attention focused on the car door's handle. Her muscles tensed further.

Please don't let us blow up in my Honda.

But nothing went *kaboom* when the deputy opened the door wide.

Alyssa let out a breath she didn't know she'd been holding.

"Okay, well, if it's a bomb it's not connected to the door," he pointed out. He moved closer to inspect the space between the seat and him. "I can't see anything here." He met her gaze. "I'm going to try to look under your seat now, okay?"

Alyssa nodded, even though she was already trying to do the logistics of that in her head. She was on the shorter side and had her seat closer to the dash because of it. Which meant Caleb Foster was about to get really close to her.

He dropped to his knees on the concrete, braced himself with one hand on the inside of the door and then very slowly hunched over so that his head was near the floorboard. Alyssa felt his breath against her bare legs as he moved between them to get a better view.

The most irrational fear that she'd missed a spot while shaving flitted through her head. When Caleb popped back up after only a few seconds, she wondered if she really had. His expression was the definition of neutral.

"So, was I being ridiculous?" she asked, hopeful.

But that ray-of-sunshine feeling lasted only an instant.

Deputy Foster pulled out his phone, but he took a moment to look directly into her eyes.

"I need you to keep doing what you're doing a little longer, okay?" he said, tone calm.

"You want me to keep sitting still," Alyssa spelled out, just to make sure they were on the same page.

Deputy Foster nodded.

Before she could stop it, her breathing went off the rails. It was one thing to think there was a bomb beneath your seat while also thinking you were being a bit insane. It was another for a man of the law to tell you to keep sitting perfectly still.

It was real now.

"So there *is* a bomb under my seat?" she asked around two short breaths.

"There's something under your seat, yes," he hedged.

"But is it a bomb?"

"I don't know for sure, but—"

Alyssa sucked in a breath and had the deepest urge to grab the man by the collar of his shirt. "You answer me right now, Deputy Foster. Do you think there's a bomb beneath my seat or not?"

He seemed surprised by her outburst, but who could blame her?

This time the deputy didn't hedge.

"Yes," he said. "I do. Which is why I need you to keep calm until we can deal with this. Okay?"

Despite his answer Alyssa decided to panic. Or, at least, her body did. The heavy air in the car, the heat of the day and the sheer thought of having survived a gunshot to the back only to be blown up in a parking lot were all too much to take. Her heartbeat wasn't just galloping anymore—it was full-out trying to exceed the speed of light. Its pursuit was having a chain reaction on what was left of her calm. Her breathing was no longer erratic. It was rushed, clumsy and impossible to conquer. It was starting to make her vision blur.

The urge to swipe her glasses off and completely freak was escalating. She wanted to try to scramble out of the car and escape the heat and fear that were tripling at an alarming rate. If the deputy hadn't been between Alyssa and the door, she might have attempted an escape plan.

But the deputy *was* there.

And his eyes were enough to hold her in place long enough for his words to reach her.

"Alyssa," he said, moving as close to her as he could without making contact. "From what I've heard, you've handled a lot worse than this." His lips quirked up into a grin. "All you have to do right now is sit still, okay? You think you can handle just sitting?"

The way he said the last part, like he was looking down on her for her worry, made something snap within her. Like he was the parent and she was a child who was being ridiculous. She took a deep breath, exhaled and took another one before she answered.

"Yes, *Deputy*," she said with a little too much attitude. "I think I can handle it."

Deputy Foster's grin grew.

It made her feel better. If only for a moment.

"I'm going to take a few pictures and then I'm going to make a lot of calls," he said.

"You aren't going to leave, are you?" she asked, already panicked at the thought.

The deputy shook his head. "I want you to know one thing for certain, Miss Garner. I *will not* leave you."

Alyssa hadn't realized how good that promise would sound.

But, boy, did it sound good!

THIRTY MINUTES.

That was all it took for all hell to break loose.

True to his word, the deputy had made several phone calls after he snapped a picture of the *maybe-but-probably* bomb. He'd done it far enough from the car so that she couldn't hear what was said—no doubt, his intention—but not far enough that Alyssa felt alone. Because, also true to his word, he didn't leave her.

Not even when the bomb squad showed up and confirmed the *maybe-but-probably* bomb was in fact a *probably-and-definitely* bomb. Though the head of the squad, a towering man named Charlie, encouraged the deputy to clear the area while they assessed options.

Options.

That was a word that might have brought Alyssa a sense of hope, or even fear, if she wasn't baking alive. The day had gone from hot to hell and she was stuck in a vacuum of it. She no longer had the energy to panic. All of that had left her body in waves of sweat, adhering every article of clothing she was wearing to her like a second skin.

And yet the deputy kept coming back.

Along with Charlie, who was now suited up with a helmet and clear mask in front of his face to boot. He lifted it to address Alyssa directly.

"Miss Garner, how are you doing?"

"I'm okay," she lied.

Deputy Foster raised his eyebrow.

"Alyssa, how are you doing?" he repeated with a tone that reminded her of a parent. She managed a defeated sigh.

"I think I might pass out soon," she admitted. "It's getting really hard to breathe."

If this alarmed the deputy, he didn't show it. In fact, neither man did. Which meant she probably looked as bad as she felt and they had been expecting it. The cold water she'd had through a straw hadn't been enough. Just like the fan that had been set up next to the car. It had only pushed the heat toward her. In no way did it alleviate the temperature she was currently suffering through.

"Then why don't we get you out of here?" Charlie said.

"That would be nice," she responded. Picturing a bathtub filled with ice cubes with her name on it. Forget about citrus bath salts.

A man she didn't recognize walked up to the car and cleared his throat.

"Can I have a moment, sir?" he asked Charlie.

He nodded, flashed a quick smile to Alyssa and then walked off. Again, she couldn't hear what was discussed, but the movement brought attention to the far end of the parking lot. It was being cleared. The staff from the courthouse, and even some people from the sheriff's department next door, were moving farther away.

Alyssa looked back at Deputy Foster. She realized he was wearing a bomb vest. "So, do they think they can really get me out of here?"

The deputy followed her gaze to his vest. He straightened it and then lowered himself to meet her stare head-on.

"I'll be honest with you," he started. "I don't know them personally, but the sheriff and Captain Jones both say Charlie and his team are the best in the South." He cut another grin. "And they think they're going to get you out of this with all limbs attached, so I'm going to bet on a yes."

Alyssa gave the smallest of nods. Her vision was starting to blur a little. She tried to pull in a calming breath. The air was so wet she felt like she was drowning.

"Hey, listen to me," he continued, tone tough. Stern. "When they get you out of here, how about I take you out for a nice jug of sweet tea? That's something you guys seem to like around here, right? Sweet tea?"

Despite everything, Alyssa snorted.

"You must be from up north," she muttered, each word strained.

She watched as his look of concern seemed to grow. Then, altogether, he began to blur.

"Alyssa," he said, voice raised. "All you have to do is sit still. You got that?"

"I'm trying," she defended. To her own ears she sounded breathless. And not in that sexy Scarlett O'Hara way.

Charlie swam back into view a few seconds later. His mask was down now. He turned to the deputy. "I guess if your captain *and* sheriff can't make you leave, then I shouldn't try either."

The deputy shook his head. At least, that was what Alyssa thought he did. Either way, when Charlie was addressing her, Deputy Foster was still there.

It was comforting.

"Okay, Miss Garner, I'm going to very slowly try to replace your weight with this metal plate," he said, already going into the back seat, the only way to reach the bomb. Which made her a little happier, considering she didn't think her floorboard could accommodate the big man like it had the deputy. "When we've done that successfully, then Deputy Foster here will take you somewhere much cooler."

"O-Okay."

The world around her was becoming one giant blur. Alyssa wanted to watch what Charlie was doing. She wanted to ask questions. She wanted to tell Deputy Foster to go where it was safe. But the fact of the matter was, Alyssa was putting all the energy she had left into not passing out.

CALEB WAS SWEATING BULLETS.

He split his focus between Charlie trying to fool the bomb by thinking Alyssa was still sitting on top of it and the woman herself. Since the water and fan hadn't worked, she'd spent almost forty-five minutes being drained, and now he wasn't sure if she'd make it past another minute.

Her head was leaning back against the headrest, and her eyelids seemed to be fighting gravity. Caleb wanted to touch her, to remind her he was there, but he couldn't. Not just because of the bomb. While he was starting to get an idea of her character, she still had no idea about his.

And he wanted to keep it that way.

"Okay. Here we go. Get ready to grab her," Charlie commanded. "I think I've— What the hell?"

Alyssa must have really been out of it. She didn't look alarmed in the slightest at the sharp tone the man trying to disarm the bomb beneath her took on.

But Caleb did. "What's go—"

Click.

"Damn," Charlie interrupted. "Grab her!"

Click. Click.

"Grab her now," Charlie yelled again, struggling out of the back seat in his uniform.

Caleb didn't have to be told a third time.

He threaded his arms beneath Alyssa's legs and back and hoisted her out in one quick move.

Click.

Charlie was already yelling, "Now run!"

Caleb tucked Alyssa against his chest and ran faster than he'd ever run before.

"Eight seconds," Charlie yelled out to anyone who could hear.

Like ants in the rain, everyone in front of or behind the blocked-off perimeter of the parking lot scurried this way and that, trying to get as far away as they could. The crowd that had formed was yelling while deputies and bomb squad alike were barking orders to each other and bystanders.

Two members of the squad in particular stood out. Instead of running away from the car, they were running toward Caleb, Alyssa and Charlie with two dark blankets. When the five of them finally collided, Charlie yelled to hit the ground.

Caleb dove onto his side so he would take the brunt of the fall, and then just as quickly rolled over to cover the woman in his arms. The bomb squad men positioned themselves on either side of Charlie and Caleb and threw the blankets—which Caleb now realized were bomb blankets, made from layers of Kevlar— over each of them.

Caleb felt like he was being pulled every which way in the moments that followed. What-ifs sprang up in his mind like flowers in the spring—What if they hadn't cleared the blast area? What if the bomb blanket didn't help them? What if he never got to take Alyssa out for that drink of sweet tea he'd offered?—while his body seemed to be running on instinct. It created a cage around the woman, trying to make itself as big as possible to protect her at all costs. But then another part of him, one he didn't know where it was coming from, was looking down at her face—slack from the unconsciousness she finally had given in to—and thinking how beautiful she was. But then everyone was yelling and he remembered to fear what was about to happen.

Not for himself, but for Alyssa.

Chapter Six

They waited.

And waited.

And waited.

No explosion rocked the ground, filled the air or even disrupted the birds chirping in the distance. Caleb chanced a look over to Charlie, who gave him nothing less than a similar expression of confusion.

"When I slid the plate in, a counter slid out for ten seconds," he defended. "It started to count down instantly. It should have gone off by now."

Cautiously both men stood, Caleb scooping Alyssa back up and putting her firmly against his chest. "I'm getting her out of here."

Charlie didn't stop him and ordered one of the bomb squad with the bomb blankets to follow until they made it past the barricade.

"Thanks, man," Caleb made sure to say. The man nodded.

"No problem," he answered. "It's my job."

The simple statement was all it took to remind Caleb

of his own job. If he still had one. As if he'd been summoned, Captain Jones was at their side.

"I told the EMTs to stay farther back, just in case," he hurried, pointing out the ambulance on the other side of the street. There was a news van a few yards from it, despite the blocks that had been put between them. A cameraman and a woman wielding a microphone were standing tall and ready. "Let me take care of them. You follow—"

Both men paused as a foreign sound filled the air.

"Is that—" the captain started, turning around to look in the direction of Alyssa's car. Caleb did the same. "—music?" he finished.

The world quieted around them. Bystanders, deputies and bomb squad alike became silent and listened. There was no mistaking it. Coming from the abandoned Honda wasn't fire and smoke but music.

A piano solo.

What was going on?

Alyssa stirred in Caleb's arms. It brought him out of his moment of wonder. "Time to get you out of here."

ALYSSA WISHED SHE'D worn a nicer bra. The one she had on now was off-beige, comfortable, did its job and was *not* supposed to be seen by anyone other than herself. Her panties—black, not beige, also comfortable and just as capable of doing their job—were on the same list of Things That Were Very Private. And yet, looking down at herself, there they were. Open to the hospital room around her just as they had been open to the

EMTs who had deemed it necessary to strip her down in the ambulance.

Sure, they were trying to bring her core temperature down as quickly as possible to save her brain cells from dying off and, well, her dying off too. Yet there she was, all brain cells intact, remembering that it hadn't just been her and the EMTs in the ambulance.

Deputy Caleb Foster had been there too.

Fresh heat crawled up Alyssa's neck and into her cheeks. No one would count it as embarrassment, seeing as how she'd spent the last half hour being treated for heat stroke. Still, when someone knocked on the door, she tried to mentally restrain the blush.

"Hello?" a woman called. "My name is Cassie Gates. I'm from the sheriff's department. May I come in?"

The name was familiar to Alyssa, but she couldn't quite place how.

"You may," she responded, grabbing the thin sheet and holding it loosely over her body. Part of her treatment had allowed her to stay in her own undergarments but nothing else, minus several ice packs strategically placed against her skin. Which was a big reason Deputy Foster had excused himself. Though, she realized later, that was only after the doctor had said they believed she'd be fine.

A blond-haired woman around Alyssa's age came in and shut the door behind her. She was dressed in a pale pink blouse, khaki skirt and sandals. Not what Alyssa expected when she'd said "sheriff's department."

"I hope I'm not intruding too much," she greeted, coming forward with her hand outstretched. "They told me you were a bit indisposed until your temperature was back to normal."

"No, it's fine," Alyssa assured her, shaking. She motioned to a chair next to the bed. "There's already been quite a few people who have seen me today. I'll take good health over modesty any day."

The woman smiled and took a seat. The movement shifted some of her hair to the side. In the middle of her neck was a nasty, circular scar. Alyssa brought her eyes back up to Cassie's in a flash. She hoped her stray in attention wasn't noticed.

"So, you're from the sheriff's department?"

Cassie nodded. If she noticed Alyssa noticing the scar, she didn't comment on it.

"I'm one of the dispatchers," she explained. "Currently working night shift."

Alyssa still didn't understand why a dispatcher with the sheriff's department had come to see her.

"And you're probably wondering why I of all people am here right now," Cassie added with a laugh.

Alyssa joined in.

"Not to be rude, but yes, I was wondering that a little," she admitted.

"I don't blame you," Cassie assured her. She moved to the edge of her seat and clasped her hands across her lap. "I'm actually here because of several different reasons, the first being I'm a woman and Captain Jones thought it would be more appropriate if I was the one to check in with you." She held up her hand to stop whatever comment Alyssa had. "While there are several women throughout our department, I think he *actually* chose me because I was in your position somewhat last year." She moved her hand up to motion to the scar on her neck. "I think he wants you to be able to talk to someone who knows what it's like to be going about your day and then in a flash everything changes."

It finally clicked for Alyssa.

"The man who shot inside the department last year," she remembered. That story had been on all the news outlets for weeks after it happened, including the woman who had been shot in the neck. It had been because of a case the sheriff had been working then. Though the rest of the details were harder to recall.

"When I woke up that morning, I didn't imagine I'd be taking a bullet," Cassie confirmed. "Which is why I think Captain Jones thought of me to check on you."

"Because, not only did I not plan on sitting on a bomb today, I also didn't plan on taking a bullet last year either," Alyssa guessed.

Cassie nodded. "I may not be a therapist, but I am a fellow trauma survivor." She cut a grin. "I'm relatable!"

Alyssa couldn't help laughing. It felt good. She eased the sheet off her, no longer worried about the other woman seeing her exposed skin. "So you're here to see if I'm coping with everything that's happened?" she asked when both had sobered.

Cassie nodded. "Basically."

Alyssa had already spent her slight isolation in the last half hour wondering about that same thing. One person could only take so much, but she'd come to the conclusion that she wasn't at her breaking point. Not yet, at least.

"I'm doing okay," she answered. "I'm more confused than anything. I don't understand who would put a bomb in my car or why. Especially one that just played music, like Deputy Foster said. What's the point?"

Cassie shrugged.

"Some people don't think like we'd expect them to, but I assure you the sheriff's department will get to the bottom of the who at the very least." Cassie held up her index finger. "Which brings me to another bit of business. Sheriff Reed along with Chief Deputy Simmons wanted me to express their deepest apologies that they aren't here in person to help with the investigation. They are working another investigation that has become hard to break away from. But the sheriff wanted to assure you—and I do too—that Captain Jones and the rest of the department are more than capable."

Alyssa felt better at the sheriff's words, even if they were funneling through someone else. She had been one of the many residents of Riker County who had elected him to office. She was also a closet fan of his wife's because of the fund-raising event she and her business partner had put together to help the victims' families in the wake of the bank robbery. The couple's kindness, as well as the department's, had shone through during a dark time in the community. Alyssa trusted them, even if some of them weren't actually in town.

"Thank you," she said. "I just want the trial to be over and everything to go back to normal."

"It will," Cassie promised. She started to stand. Her demeanor flipped. Her smile turned mischievous. "Now, before I go to work, I wanted to give you a little advice." She walked closer and lowered her voice. Alyssa leaned in, curious. The ice pack on her stomach shifted. "Ask specifically for Deputy Foster to take you home when the time comes. If you want to help him out, that is."

Another thought Alyssa wouldn't share with the woman was how she'd already decided it would be his help she asked for. Considering that he had risked being blown up to save her, she wanted the chance to truly thank him. So far she hadn't gotten any alone time with him since she'd been brought in. Still, she wondered why Cassie had brought it up. "Why does he need help?"

Cassie's playful mood depleted. Her smile disappeared.

"He's new and not the easiest man to work with," she said. "His position wasn't helped when he defied several direct orders today."

"He defied direct orders?"

"To leave you and let the professionals handle the dismantling themselves," she answered, apologetic. "It sounds harsh, but it's protocol. And, well, that's not the first time he's overstepped his duties during his career."

Cassie's eyes widened and her face flushed. Alyssa had a feeling she hadn't meant to say as much as she had.

"Either way, I thought that maybe you asking for him specifically would remind everyone else that there are exceptions, even to protocol."

Her smile was back. She did a little nod to Alyssa and started to leave.

"Hey, Cassie," Alyssa called. The woman turned, face open and still smiling. "Getting shot…" Alyssa paused while she looked for the words she hadn't realized she needed to say, to relate with someone else. The spot on her back felt like it was burning again. Finally she settled on simple. "It sure does suck, doesn't it?"

Cassie didn't miss a beat. "It sure does."

"THEY'RE SAYING IT was a joke."

Caleb looked up from his chair and at the water bottle Deputy Dante Mills had outstretched.

Caleb was mad. "Then whoever *they* is has one hell of a sense of humor."

Dante shook the bottle again. Caleb finally took it. He'd already downed a few since they'd come to the hospital.

"I'm not arguing with that."

He quieted as Caleb took a drink. He'd noticed that Dante had often given him time to let his thoughts, and mood, settle while they were patrolling together. It was a much different situation than what he'd dealt with on the force in Portland. While he never had just one partner, it seemed that everyone he did get matched up with fought to keep the conversation going. Even when it was clear he didn't want it to. Either way, he was usually grateful for the quiet.

However, at the moment, it wasn't helping calm him down. Not after the morning he'd had.

"No one thinks that it's connected to the Storm Chasers' trial?" Caleb snapped. "I mean, it's one hell of a coincidence it happens after the fire alarm was destroyed. Which we conveniently don't have any security camera footage for, I might add."

"The last I heard, Captain Jones and Police Chief Hawser were discussing the possibility of a connection, but there's not enough to go on yet to make any real claim."

"Other than 'some people' think it's a joke," Caleb deadpanned.

Dante held his hands up in defense.

"Hey, man, I'm just telling you what people are thinking," he said. "You're not the most loved guy around here—seemingly of your own choosing, which is fine, you do you—so I'm trying to keep you in the loop here."

Caleb wanted to retaliate with a barrage of "you don't know me" and "I don't need your help or pity" sentiments, but for once, he let it lie. Because Dante wasn't exactly wrong. Instead the deputy's words rolled into a silence that he waited a few moments to break.

"Listen, I just wanted you to know what's going on," Dante continued. "And not just because I know you a little bit better than the rest of the department, but because of what you did today. Took guts."

At this, Caleb snorted.

"I don't think the captain or sheriff appreciate my 'guts,'" he mused. He'd been on the receiving end of some heated words from Captain Jones for disobeying a direct order.

Dante nudged Caleb's shoulder. "Well, I know one person who does."

Caleb followed his gaze down the hall behind him.

Captain Jones had his head bent and his brow pulled together as he talked and walked along with a woman.

Caleb wasn't sure what reaction he'd expected to feel when he saw Alyssa again, but whatever he was currently feeling he couldn't quite place. Even when she brought those startlingly blue eyes up to meet his.

However, that feeling went away when Captain Jones swung his stare toward him.

"Ruh roh," Dante said beneath his breath. They both stood tall and ready. Before Alyssa or Jones could reach them, Dante added an afterthought. "Remember to be nice," he whispered.

"Good to see you up and moving around." Dante greeted Alyssa before the captain could get his, no doubt, hit in at Caleb.

"Thanks," Alyssa said with a smile. It was amazing how much better she looked from earlier that day. Then again, the AC in the hospital was no joke. The silver lining, at least, to having to be there at all. "I still would love to shower and get some fresh clothes, but I'm not going to complain, since it could have been worse."

Her eyes flashed to Caleb's. He kept quiet. Jones did not.

"Which brings me to the what-happens-next," he began. "I've told Miss Garner here that the bomb squad has finished its search of her residence and come up empty. Still, I'd like to keep a law enforcement presence around her until we can find this man with the glasses you both have described or another lead."

Caleb felt his jaw tighten. He wanted to volunteer, but seeing as how his last conversation with Jones had gone, he was sure that he would only dig his proverbial grave deeper with the man.

"Miss Garner has agreed to this suggestion, and—" Jones took a noticeable pause to draw in a deep breath. Frustration. "—has requested that that deputy be you, Mr. Foster."

"If that's okay," she hurried to add. "You've already done more than enough, thinking you were risking your life to keep me, a stranger, company." Her eyes flickered over to the captain. "It was brave and selfless."

The captain gave a tight nod. His smile was tighter. A muscle twitched at his jaw. Caleb felt his eyebrow rise. Was she pleading his case in a not-so-subtle way to the captain?

"It was no problem," Caleb assured her. "And if it's okay with the captain, then that's fine by me."

Captain Jones brandished a forced smile. "Who am I to bench such a brave and selfless man?"

Chapter Seven

"I think my love for cars is now forever tainted."

Alyssa gave Caleb what she hoped was a humorous expression, not one that reflected the anxiety that had begun to well up inside her at the mere sight of his car.

"Or at least the seats," she added with a little laugh. Just beneath her surface, her already tired muscles were tensed.

Her car might not have been the most reliable vehicle—it was over a decade old and had the rust and wear to prove it—but at the end of the day it was hers. To have someone go plant a bomb, fake or not, inside it felt a little too intimate. She had, admittedly, felt upset when Captain Jones told her it had been transported to a different site where CSI and bomb squad could take a better look at it. Captain Jones assured her she'd get it back in a day, two tops. Still, with nerves twirling in her stomach like a majorette's baton, she knew her days of carelessly sliding into any car would be met with a good dollop of anxiety. Her car especially.

And she hated that.

Caleb settled in behind the wheel and looked

through the opened door out at her. He motioned to the passenger's seat, unflinching. "Don't worry. When I came down to turn the AC on while you were talking to the captain, I made sure to look beneath all the seats. No bombs, real or otherwise, in this car. I promise."

She kept her fake smile in place and covertly let out an exhale of relief. Soon she was buckled in and they were pulling away from the hospital. The trip had been another unwelcome surprise to a day she'd never expected to live through.

Alyssa was glad to see the hospital move to their rearview as they drove toward her house. With close to no interaction with him, she pointed out which streets the deputy needed to take. The lunch traffic was tapering off, but it was still congested in some parts and slowed their progress. The quiet that had taken over the car intensified. It made her uncomfortable. Or, rather, the time it gave her to think did. By the time they hit the intersection that guided them toward her neighborhood and had to wait through two more lights, Alyssa was nearly out of her mind. So she tried to alleviate the heaviness of memories starting to weigh down on her by talking.

"I don't like hospitals," she admitted.

The deputy cut her a look. It made her feel silly for blurting out the first thought that had popped into her head.

"I think that's a universal truth," he said. "Show me someone who loves hospitals and I'll show you a liar."

Alyssa had to agree with that. "I suppose you're right. I guess I should say my last experience with one was…" She paused, looking for a word that expressed terror mixed with confusion but still polite for everyday conversation. *"…unsettling."*

No sooner had she said it than Alyssa realized she had no idea if the man next to her knew what had happened the year before. At least not to the extent of her personal injuries. While she was in the car that morning, they hadn't spoken about anything personal.

"I was hurt during the bank robbery last year and woke up in the hospital," she hurriedly explained. "Law enforcement referred to me as a victim, while the doctor and nurse referred to me as a survivor. And all I wanted to know was how I'd gotten there and how badly I was hurt. It was all very…" She paused to look for another word to describe such a heavy feeling.

"Unsettling," Deputy Foster offered. Alyssa nodded. "Was today the first time you've been back after the robbery? If you don't mind my asking."

Again, Alyssa nodded.

"At least this time I woke up beforehand," she said. A fresh wave of heat moved through her cheeks. "Though it was definitely an experience to wake up to my clothes being taken off in an ambulance. Again, definitely not how I saw my day going."

Deputy Foster kept his eyes on the street. Alyssa felt her blush cranking up the heat. Again she found herself wishing she'd worn a different bra and panty set.

"The EMTs were pretty quick with it too," he said, eyes still averted. "I turned away one second and in the next they were handing me your clothes." He shrugged.

"But they assured me that they were used to dealing with heat exhaustion and knew what they were doing."

Alyssa patted the buttons on her blouse. "I am impressed they didn't rip anything. I already lost my favorite shirt last year."

The deputy chuckled but didn't respond past that. Alyssa decided to steer clear of any more hospital talk while silently saying a thank-you to the powers that be. At least this time she hadn't died in between the ambulance ride and the ER.

Carpenter was small but not small enough where there weren't a handful of heavily populated neighborhoods in and around the town. Alyssa lived in one named the Meadows, closer to the town limits. The houses were older and, at times, funkier than the traditional ones in other parts of the town. She liked to believe it was an infusion of character and not simply houses that were in desperate need of renovating.

"So, this is me," she said, pointing to her house at the end of a cul-de-sac. Again she thought of the word *character* as he pulled into the driveway of the two-story.

"Nice house," he said, not cutting the engine off. She wondered what his plan was but couldn't find the courage to ask. He was still a stranger, despite their shared morning.

"Thanks. My sister calls it the jigsaw house. It's a work in progress, on the inside, that is. I've been slowly remodeling it since I moved in. The previous owners had a hard love for 1970s-style wallpaper and green tile. Almost every room looks different from the others."

Deputy Foster switched his gaze back to the house and nodded. His talkative levels were plummeting. And she didn't know why. One of his hands rested lazily on the steering wheel, the other on his lap. He seemed bored.

"Okay," she rallied. "Well, thanks again for everything. I can't imagine how I would have handled everything without you there earlier."

Alyssa fumbled for the door handle. Her embarrassment made the space between them seem so small. She was itching to get inside the house.

"No need to thank me. I was just doing my job."

He turned off the engine but didn't move a muscle.

Alyssa hesitated. A part of her wanted to invite the man inside—it was the least she could do—but the way he was acting ignited her self-preservation.

"I'll be out here if you need me."

A new hardness edged its way into his tone as he said it. One that spoke of finality. Alyssa finally got a hold on the handle and let herself out. Her muscles whined at the quick movement, but her blush compelled her to keep the pace until she was at her front door. It wasn't until she was in the privacy of her bedroom that she wondered what the deputy was thinking.

Because the man she'd just left wasn't the same man who had promised he wouldn't leave her that morning.

NIGHT WAS CREEPING around the car before the porch light clicked on. Caleb had been listening to the frogs chirping like insects for the last half hour. Before that he'd focused on the birds. And before that he'd been thinking about him being an idiot.

If Alyssa hadn't requested him to guard her, Caleb would have volunteered, no doubt about that in his mind. Yet as soon as he'd seen the fear—the vulnerability—that had overtaken her outside his car in the hospital parking lot, he'd remembered his one rule while in Riker County.

Don't get attached.

So he'd shut down. Spoken only when spoken to and kept things professional. Yet he couldn't deny that he'd wanted to know more about her. And it was that feeling that had only strengthened his resolve to stay in the car.

Even though he'd wanted to go inside.

Now, after his resolution had hardened, Alyssa stepped onto the front porch and turned her gaze directly to his. She'd dressed down in the few hours that had passed since he saw her, wearing a white T-shirt and jeans. Her hair was wet and dark, pulled back at the nape of her neck, and her glasses were off. She was squinting. It compelled him to step outside his car.

"Is everything okay?" he asked.

Alyssa adjusted her gaze. It was still a little off. It made him wonder how blind she was without her glasses.

"Um, actually, this is kind of embarrassing." She shifted her weight from one foot to the other. "But could you give me a hand? I kind of..." She said the last part so low Caleb started toward her.

"Say that again?"

Alyssa shifted her weight again. She was embarrassed, that was clear. It intrigued Caleb even further. He was already at the steps when she spoke up.

"I kind of lost my glasses," she repeated. She let out a long sigh. "In the attic."

It was so unexpected that Caleb's rule of staying away from the woman took a back seat. "Okay, you're going to have to explain that one."

Alyssa's cheeks noticeably reddened. She motioned for him to follow her. "Remember how I said the inside of the house is like a jigsaw?"

"Yeah."

"The attic is more of an endless maze."

She shut the door behind him and motioned up the stairs. Just from where Caleb was standing in the entryway, he could already agree with Alyssa's sister's nickname for the place. The stairs were oak but had a thick green carpet runner, while the tile they were standing on was a multicolored mosaic design. Of what, he couldn't tell, but it was definitely different.

"The second story isn't as dramatic," she promised, guessing at his thoughts. "Just some *funky* wallpaper I've been avoiding. The shag carpet, however, officially died right after I moved in."

She led him up the stairs into a hall that opened up to one guest bedroom, one bathroom and he assumed the master suite. He couldn't help pausing at the open door to the closest bedroom.

"Well, you weren't lying about the funky part."

There was bright-orange-striped wallpaper as far as the eye could see. If he had a weekend, he could tear it all out, no problem. Then they could paint it something less intense and headache inducing.

They.

That had popped up out of nowhere.

"It's a work in progress," she continued, unaware that he'd just mentally coupled them. "The attic, though. It's stuck in its ways."

"And can I ask why you were up there and how you lost your glasses?"

He followed her to the ladder in the middle of the hallway. Instead of going up, she hesitated and turned to face him.

"Short story, everything that happened today got me feeling…" She paused, seemingly looking for the right words. Her eyebrows drew together and her lips turned down in a frown. Those lips. He'd noticed them while hovering over her waiting for a bomb to go off. Pink and bare.

"Nostalgic," she supplied, holding up her hands. "I know that sounds strange, but when I was in the hospital, right after what happened at the bank, my sister, Gabby, took a leave at work to help me while I recovered. We were really close growing up and she lives in Colorado, so it was the longest we had seen each other in a while. And it was nice." She smiled. Those distracting lips stretching wide. "Today got me thinking about what happened then, which got me thinking about Gabby and, well, that snowballed into thinking about my parents." She laughed and pointed to the ceiling. "And I was trying to get to a particularly difficult box with photo albums in them when my glasses dropped out of sight."

"And you're one of those people who *really* can't see without your glasses," he guessed.

It earned him a laugh.

"Blind as a bat," she answered. "I tried feeling around for them but for the life of me couldn't find them." That blush was back, showing up against her skin in a flash. It surprised Caleb.

And intrigued him.

"So I should probably go up first just in case," he said with a laugh. She nodded.

"If you don't mind. I'm not a fan of contacts and would really like to not break my current pair of glasses." She groaned, blush burning bright. "Because I kind of already lost my only spare."

Caleb couldn't help continuing to laugh.

It in turn grabbed a giggle from her. "Armed robberies and fake bombs? I can be smooth. Any other time? Not so much."

"Being good under pressure isn't a bad thing," he pointed out.

"But having your glasses fall off your face into oblivion isn't either."

He couldn't argue with that.

They climbed the ladder and began the great attic search, as Alyssa dubbed it after several minutes had gone by without any luck. The space was roomy and easy to stand up in, but thanks to boxes, old furniture and awkwardly shaped decorations, navigating around wasn't the easiest thing to do.

"I just have to ask," Caleb finally said, after pushing aside another box like he was directing a game of Tetris. "Do you have a box in here that leads to Narnia maybe? Because I—"

"Ah!"

Caleb shot up from the crouched position he'd been in just as Alyssa danced, twirled and then flung herself toward him. He met her halfway between their original spots just as she grabbed the hem of her shirt.

"Spider," she shrieked. *"Spider!"*

Without wasting any time, Alyssa yanked up on her shirt and pulled it clear over her head like it was on fire. She threw it across the attic. Caleb watched in awe as the T-shirt soared through the air and fell out of sight through the open attic door. Still, the woman was not satisfied.

"Is it on me?" she yelled, flapping her arms in the air. Her terror had its claws in her so deep that she didn't seem to realize she'd just stripped down in front of him. Wearing a white lace bra, definitely not the beige one from earlier in the ambulance, she kept flailing around with fervor. The motion might have helped her with the bug problem, but it wasn't helping with his concentration.

"Hold still," he ordered, trying his best not to laugh. He reached out to grab her by the arms. It was the only way to keep her in place when it was clear she wasn't listening.

"Is it still on me?" she repeated, voice pitching high.

Caleb did a cursory look at her chest and stomach,

actively trying not to scan too closely, before turning her around.

His stomach dropped.

Thoughts of spiders and lace bras and lost glasses were blanketed by a wide puckering of skin.

A scar.

The one that Dupree Slater had given her.

Caleb had seen his fair share of gunshot wounds and scars during his career with law enforcement, but this one was different. Angry. The scar *looked* angry. Violent, even. Just like the man who had left it.

It made *him* angry in turn.

During his lifetime, Caleb had learned to stop asking the motive of why some people did what they did. But right now, feeling the warmth of Alyssa against his hands and staring at her bare skin, he couldn't help asking that question.

Why would someone do anything to hurt this woman?

"Well?" Alyssa asked, voice still raised. It dislodged his anger. Though he had no doubt there would be a dark aftertaste for a while in its wake. "I'm still blind here."

"There's nothing on you," he answered. Even to his ears his voice had gone cold. He tried to adjust it to something lighter. "I think your new dance moves shook it free."

Alyssa stopped her panicked routine and let out a deep, shuddering breath. She turned back to face him.

"I felt it drop on me and then just saw this blur against my shirt," she said, shaking her head. The movement once again shook the rest of her. Caleb made sure to keep his eyes above her chest. "I can't handle spiders."

Another shudder racked her body.

He lowered his hands from her arms. And tried to ignore how pink her lips still looked.

Caleb cleared his throat.

"Not that I'm complaining about the view—" he started. He didn't have to finish the statement. He couldn't help smiling as Alyssa finally realized what she'd done. Her arms slapped across her chest in a flash. A blush that put all the other blushes of the day to shame ran across her face in an instant.

"Oh my God," she breathed.

Caleb averted his gaze completely, already turning, when something caught his eye.

"Well, look at that." He walked a few feet away to an overturned box, one of a handful of casualties of Alyssa's panicked dance. "Too bad a spider couldn't have fallen on you sooner." He bent over and picked up her glasses. There was no telling where they'd been before she started flailing around.

"Thank goodness!" She shied as far away from him as she could while still grabbing the black frames from him. Once they were back to their rightful place, she tightened her arms around herself. She didn't meet his gaze as she looked around the immediate area. "Now, how about my shirt?"

Caleb laughed.

He was about to give her the news that it was no

longer in the attic when the ladder leading to the hall-way beneath them creaked under someone's weight.

This time Alyssa met his stare.

One emotion was written clearly across her face.

Fear.

Chapter Eight

One moment Alyssa was standing next to the deputy and in the next he was in front of her, gun out and raised.

It happened so fast that she temporarily forgot her lapse in sanity that had led to her stripping off her shirt and then demanding the man take a look at her. That embarrassment was sucked straight out as another long creak sounded on the steps. Someone was definitely climbing up.

The deputy squared his shoulders, tightened his stance and waited.

A dark bald head popped into view, followed by a truly alarmed face.

"Robbie!"

Alyssa reached out and grabbed the deputy's shoulder.

"He's a friend," she hurried, but he was already lowering his gun.

Robbie's eyes were wide as he looked between them. The deputy holstered his gun and took a step back, blocking Robbie's view of her bare skin. Still, they all knew he'd seen enough to know she wasn't wearing her shirt.

A fact the man already knew, given that he was holding it in his hands.

"Do you always walk around unannounced, Mr. Rickman?" Caleb asked, tone dry.

"We knocked and when no one answered we got worried," he defended. "We used the spare key Alyssa gave us."

Eleanor's voice floated up, but Alyssa couldn't make it out. Maybe it was the mortification that was setting in.

"Could you throw me that?" she cut in, motioning to the shirt.

"I guess it's not my business to ask why it was down here?" Robbie tossed it over. Caleb caught it and passed it back without looking. Alyssa hurriedly put it back on.

"There was a spider," the deputy deadpanned.

Robbie held up a hand.

"Say no more," he said. "If she's anything like Eleanor when she sees a lizard, then you're lucky to be alive, son." Caleb's demeanor loosened. He snorted. "Okay, well, unless you kids are busy, we brought some food over for supper. And by some food I mean a lot of food."

On cue Alyssa's stomach growled.

Caleb thrust his thumb back at her. "I think that's her answer."

Robbie smiled. "What about you? We brought more than enough."

Alyssa couldn't see the man's expression but was surprised when he nodded so quickly.

"If that's okay with you, that is?" Caleb turned toward her and waited.

From one moment to the next, the deputy had shifted his demeanor. Blunt to compassionate to detached and empathetic to humorous and, now, polite. He was a hard man to pin down, that was for sure. However, Alyssa couldn't deny she felt a connection. Or maybe she just wanted one.

Another flourish of heat began to make its ascent upward as she shared a look with the handsome man. She managed to nod.

"You helped me find my glasses," she pointed out, avoiding bringing up any part of the fake bomb while Robbie was within earshot. Once she had begun to normalize, Alyssa had called him and his wife to let them know what happened. Carpenter might have been a small town, but not everyone had seen the live news story when they were trying to get her out of the car. The Rickmans had been upset but promised to give her space. But now, standing in an awkward position with the deputy, she was almost thankful that their idea of "space" was waiting until supper to come over with food. "Of course you can stay and eat, Deputy."

"Why don't you call me Caleb?" he said, voice filling with a hint of grit. "I think we've both earned that, wouldn't you say?"

Alyssa felt the burn in her cheeks now. And she hated herself for it. She'd only met the man that morning and now here she was, wanting to know him.

In more ways than one.

ELEANOR DIDN'T HOLD BACK.

"Sweetie, if you keep that up you'll end up suffocating her," Robbie pointed out. "I'm pretty sure she needs to breathe."

Caleb watched as the older woman kept her arms tightly around Alyssa before finally relenting. He started to take a seat when Robbie stopped him.

"You might as well go ahead and let her get at you before you get comfortable," he warned, pointing to his wife.

Caleb raised his eyebrow.

"I didn't do anything," he tried, but apparently Mrs. Rickman wasn't having any of that. She detached from Alyssa and was on him within seconds. For a tall, slender woman she had a surprisingly viselike grip. It reminded Caleb of his mother. Which made him instantly like the woman more.

"You stood by our girl." Her brown eyes locked on his after she pulled away. "Don't sell yourself short for that," she scolded.

Caleb nodded. "Yes, ma'am."

Eleanor smiled and then turned her attention to the dining room table. It was long and narrow but in no way looked prepared to hold the spread that the Rickmans had brought over. Robbie caught his eye and shrugged.

"We Southerners are big on comforting each other with food," he explained. "Some people like flowers, some like presents, we like overgenerous portions of mashed potatoes and gravy."

Alyssa motioned to a glass container half covered in aluminum foil.

"Which can be found in this particular dish," she said with a laugh.

Caleb didn't miss the smile that sprang up on Eleanor's face at the sound. It was clear Robbie and his wife cared about Alyssa. It was also clear that she was fond of them too. Helping Robbie during the robbery had made a stranger into a friend.

And now here Caleb was, getting hugged and fed by strangers while trying to protect another.

Don't get attached, he reminded himself. His stomach growled in response.

"Here, let me suggest this." Alyssa took a seat next to him and opened a plastic container with obvious glee. Eleanor handed out plates before taking her own seat opposite them and next to her husband. They started to talk among themselves as Alyssa continued. "This is Eleanor's famous green bean casserole. If you're as hungry as I am, then this should hit the spot just right." She leaned closer to him and lowered her voice to a whisper. Caleb caught the scent of citrus off her wet hair. "But make sure you save room. I spied a few slices of homemade apple pie in the kitchen. And you definitely don't want to miss that."

Alyssa gave him a coy smile.

His inner voice chanting out his one rule quieted.

The food was good, but with Robbie and Eleanor the company was better. It wasn't long before Caleb found out just how likable the couple was.

And just how polite they remained.

No one brought up the fake bomb or the trial or asked personal questions. Instead they talked about sports, the weather, and their suggestions on how to make Alyssa's house less like a puzzle and more of a home. On that particular topic Caleb kept his opinions down to nodding to the couple's suggestions. He didn't want to intrude more than he already was doing.

It wasn't until the pie was eaten—apple, as Alyssa had promised—that the conversation took a turn. Surprisingly, it was Alyssa who drove it there.

"So, no one has called me to update me on the trial," she started. "But last I was told, a lawyer is supposed to contact me today or tomorrow about it." Her stare found Robbie's. "Do you know why?"

Robbie put down his fork. His face pinched.

"Last I heard, they were talking about having you sit out the trial," he said. "At least as a witness."

Alyssa bristled at his side.

"Sit it out?" she exclaimed. "Why?"

"The trauma of what happened. Some think you're too emotional or might make the jury more sympathetic toward you and your testimony."

"Too emotional?" Alyssa nearly yelled. "Why? Because someone played a dumb prank on me or because I'm a woman?"

Robbie held up his hands in defense.

"That's only what I heard from Ted," he said. "I don't agree with it and I don't even know if it's what's supposed to happen. I'm assuming we'll all find out tomorrow when they announce what time the trial is rescheduled for."

"Is Ted the lawyer?" Caleb butted in. Again he wished he'd researched the case and trial more after being assigned to the courthouse.

"Ted worked at the bank," Eleanor answered. "He was there when..." She cut herself off and glanced at her husband. Caleb felt stupid for not realizing earlier that what had happened at the bank had affected her just as much as the other two. She'd nearly lost her husband.

"He was also supposed to testify after Alyssa," Robbie jumped in. "They thought it would be more powerful for her to start off, considering she saw the whole thing *and* was hurt."

That surprised Caleb.

"Wait, so you aren't just a witness," he said. "You're the first."

Alyssa nodded, visibly trying to calm down.

"I was, but if someone's already talking to Ted, then it might be him now." There was anger behind her words. It was powerful, potent.

Caleb understood it.

And wanted to help it lessen.

"From what I know of what happened, even *if* you aren't able to testify, there's still a pretty cut-and-dry case against Dupree and Anna," he pointed out. "And regardless of your presence on the stand, what happened to you will still be told. Probably several times depending on what's asked of each witness."

Alyssa took a deep breath.

"I guess you're right," she said. "I just— I want them to rot in prison for the rest of their lives."

Caleb fought the urge to reach out and touch her. There wasn't much space between them as it was. It would be easy to take her hand, balled on her lap, and let her know he was there. That he was on her side. That he knew anger and how it could destroy. But he didn't.

"In my experience, people like them get what they deserve," he said instead. "Plus, I may be new, but what I know of the law enforcement in this town, and the sheriff for that matter, is they do their best to make sure justice is served."

A small smile pulled up the corners of Alyssa's lips. She nodded.

The conversation veered back into a more comforting area as they took their plates to the kitchen and cleaned up. Caleb checked the clock several times, wondering what his next play would be. Since he had been requested by Alyssa for guard duty for the day and night, Captain Jones had put Dante in his place for guard duty at the courthouse the next morning. A move that had surprised Caleb.

Captain Jones was a desk jockey and a stickler at that. Unlike Dante, he and the rest of the department hadn't shown him any special treatment. He didn't blame them, but he'd been ready to ask for it anyway.

Until Alyssa had spoken to the captain before he'd had the chance. It was against protocol, he was sure, yet the captain had obliged.

Why? he had wondered.

But now, looking at Robbie—alive and well, thanks to the woman—he could make a guess. Small towns left no room for heroics to go unnoticed. Even the sheriff's department respected what she'd done at the bank.

It made the growing foreign feeling of *needing* to protect her that much greater.

"It was good to meet you, Caleb," Eleanor said as they all filed out onto the porch. She wrapped him in a hug before he could prepare himself for it. "We're going to do this soon, so don't think we won't see each other again."

Caleb laughed. "You keep feeding me apple pie like that and I'll have dinner with you anytime."

Eleanor beamed and turned to say goodbye to Alyssa while her husband clapped him on the back.

"Thanks again for everything," Robbie said. They shook hands, but the man didn't let go right away. Instead he spoke in a whisper so the women couldn't overhear. "She's a special woman and deserves nothing but the best. You keep a good eye on her, okay?"

Caleb was quick to nod. "Yes, sir."

"Good." Robbie gave one final pump. "And maybe next time there's a 'spider' you two could put a sock on the door or something." Robbie gave him a wink and a hoot of laughter before turning to his wife and taking her hand. "It's time to go, my dear," he sang. "Wave goodbye to the young'uns!"

"I can't wave goodbye to myself," she teased.

Robbie hooted again and the two walked to the car, caught in their own bubble of mirth.

Watching them, Caleb felt an odd twinge of emotion. Regret? Desire? Grief?

He didn't know. However, it put more weight on

his current situation, standing next to Alyssa on her front porch.

"What did he say to you?" she asked, an eyebrow rising. "You're grinning."

Caleb shrugged.

"You know, just a little of this and that," he hedged. "Men talk."

She snorted. "Men talk?"

"You wouldn't understand." He felt the grin widen. It had been a long time since he'd had a good home-cooked meal. It had been even longer since he'd had even better company to share it with.

One look at Alyssa, baby blues focused solely on him, and Caleb thought he should tell her that. And thank her.

And ask when they could do it again.

Alyssa bit back a yawn.

"I'm exhausted," she said, eyes watering at the effort. Caleb ignored how that disappointed him.

"Which is my cue to get back to work," he said, already walking down the steps. "Let me know if you need anything."

"Wait, Caleb."

He should keep walking. He should go to the car and sit in it until the morning. He should ignore the pull he felt toward a woman he barely knew.

"If you're going to sit up in the driveway all night anyways, why don't you at least do it inside the house?"

Caleb turned and watched a new blush blossom across her cheeks. She scrambled to finish her thought. "I mean, I have a guest room and even a really great couch in the living room. It doesn't make sense for you to be scrunched up in a car for hours. Believe me, that's no fun."

Caleb hesitated.

He met those bright blue eyes head-on.

"You don't know me," he finally said.

However, Alyssa didn't hesitate. "I know enough." She gave him a smile. It was kind. "Please, let me do something nice for you."

He should have argued. He should have declined. He should have done a lot of things, but what he ended up doing was nodding.

And then following Alyssa Garner back into her house.

Chapter Nine

Despite being exhausted, Alyssa spent the next hour on the phone with her sister. It gave Caleb time to explore the downstairs without her by his side.

Apart from the aesthetics of floors that didn't match, walls that were covered in wallpaper from the '70s, and random bits of tile, the house was very much lived in. Books, magazines and knickknacks could be found everywhere he looked, while pictures were framed and hung with care. Caleb stopped at a few of these and tried to figure out who each person was in them, or at least, who everyone was to the woman.

The sister, Gabby, if he heard her correctly, was the easiest to spot. She made several appearances throughout the first floor. Her hair was lighter, but she had the same blue eyes. In every picture of them together, she had her arms around Alyssa. Their smiles matched too. It was contagious. It made him miss his own sister. He needed to call her soon.

Another person who was easy to connect to Alyssa was an older woman with brown hair and dark eyes but who shared the same expression as the sisters. Their mother, he guessed. She, however, wasn't in many pictures. At least not with the girls when they were older. His smile fell as he guessed she'd passed away.

Other pictures included Alyssa with people who must have been friends. Always in groups and never one-on-one. It wasn't until he was examining the frames in the living room for the third time that he realized what he was really looking for.

A boyfriend.

The day had been a rush, crazy and unexpected. In the time he'd spent with her, she'd only mentioned her sister. He'd assumed that meant there was no man in the picture. But, then again, maybe she was being private about it. Or had her own reasons not to bring him up.

Caleb's eyes stopped to rest on a collage above the fireplace. In one of the pictures, a smiling Alyssa looked out at him while two men around their age stood on either side, arms wrapped around her waist. They didn't look like her brothers.

Jealousy sprang up faster than Caleb could track it.

"I see you've found my attempt of making photo collages."

Caleb turned, surprised he hadn't heard the woman come down the stairs. He was finding that when it came to Alyssa, he wasn't always on his game. Which could be dangerous. For both of them.

"I was trying to figure out who everyone was," he admitted. He tapped the picture with the men and tried his hardest to look uninterested. "Brothers?"

He already knew they weren't but felt another pulse of jealousy when she shook her head.

"Those are the sons of Jeffries and Sons," she answered. "That's where I work. It's a small remodeling company that's local. I'm sure you would have already met them if they'd been in town. The whole family does a big cruise every year. I was invited but the trial cut into it. So they shut down the shop and now I'm getting paid vacation. *But* they, the sons, are like brothers if that counts." That satisfied Caleb more than it should have. "They even do that 'don't you hurt my sister' speech when I start dating someone. The last guy got it the worst. They sat him down and threatened bodily harm after—" Something doused her humor on the spot. Her eyebrows knitted together. Her lips thinned. It alarmed Caleb.

"After?" he prodded. Anger was already starting to burn in his chest. If any man had laid a hand on her he'd—

"After he stopped visiting me in the hospital."

"He stopped visiting you in the hospital?" he repeated. "You mean after the robbery?"

Alyssa nodded. With the motion the rest of her body seemed to fall.

"I mean, I can't blame him," she tried. "We hadn't been dating long and then suddenly I was hospital-bound and in need of hours and hours of physical therapy. It was too much for someone who already had a busy schedule." She shrugged, attempting to play off the hurt at being left when she had been most vulnerable.

Caleb didn't like that, and maybe she saw it in his expression.

Hers softened.

"It's okay," she said. Kind despite the obvious hurt. Her pink lips formed the smallest of smiles. "Not everyone stays when you want them to."

Caleb almost did several things in that moment.

He almost reached out to touch her, to comfort her, to let her know *he* was here right now. He almost turned that touch into a kiss, giving in to his curiosity about those pink, pink lips and how they felt. He almost told her that he would never have left her.

But then he realized that was exactly what he was going to do.

When he found his redemption in Riker County, he would use it to take him home.

Away from the sweltering heat and unforgiving humidity, away from the built-in familiarity between every resident, away from a department that didn't know what he was capable of, and away from the beautiful stranger standing less than a foot away from him.

So, instead, he kept quiet.

"I guess it's time for me to try to sleep," Alyssa said after the moment had passed. She didn't smile as she turned away. It wasn't until she was at the stairs that she called back to him, "Good night, Deputy."

Like an idiot he stood right where he was.

"Good night, Miss Garner."

ALYSSA SLEPT LIKE the dead.

One moment her head was touching the pillow, and the next she was waking up to someone knocking on the door. Light streamed through a gap in the curtains as she tossed the covers off her and sat up.

"Yes?" she asked, fumbling for her glasses. In the process she got caught on the cord to her cell phone charger. It fell off the night table and became a blur on the floor.

"You okay in there?" Caleb asked through the door.

For one wild second she blushed, wondering why he was outside her door, when the night before came back.

"Yeah, I'm good," she assured him, still fumbling around for her glasses. Usually she left them on the nightstand next to her phone, but for the life of her, she couldn't lay hands on them. "What time is it?" she asked, getting out of bed and searching the floor by the sides of the little table. When that search was fruitless, she got onto her knees and looked beneath the stand.

"Eight thirty," he called back.

"Eight thirty," she exclaimed, sitting up. "I'm not missing the trial, am I?"

"It was officially postponed until one this afternoon."

Alyssa let out a sigh of relief. She reached under the bed and felt around. No glasses.

How did she keep *doing* this?

"Hold on a second," she said. She grabbed her robe off the ottoman at the foot of her bed and put it over her short nightgown before opening the door. Caleb's blurry form became focused into a well-rested man dressed down in a T-shirt and jeans. "You're never going to believe this," she started, already embarrassed. "But I've—"

"You lost your glasses again?" he interrupted. He was grinning.

She nodded.

"I had them on when I got into bed so I could read a work email, but they aren't on my nightstand." Caleb's grin grew wider. "Why are you smiling like that?"

Alyssa froze as the man took a step closer. He reached up to her hair.

"Probably because they are on top of your head."

He took them off her hair. She felt heat in her cheeks.

"I can count on one hand how many times I've put them on top of my head," she said, taking them from the man and slipping them on. "And of course you get to witness one of those times. I promise I'm much more of a capable human than I let on."

Caleb laughed. It was a booming, pleasant sound. She wished she could hear more of it.

"I believe you," he assured her. "But I also believe you're just really good at losing your glasses."

"I can't disagree with you there." Once her glasses were on and she was refocused, she got down to business. "No one called me last night or this morning— unless I slept through it, of course—about the trial. I assumed it was pushed back to the afternoon."

"The results from CSU came in about the fake bomb. Whoever made it was careful, precise, but it had nothing in it that could have physically harmed you. Who put it there is still being investigated, but since the act couldn't be linked directly back to the trial, the judge thought it was pointless to delay the proceedings."

"The entire town just wants the Storm Chasers behind us," she agreed.

"Which is what's going to happen," he said. "But until then, Captain Jones needs me back at the station. I volunteered to help with the investigation since Deputy Mills took my place at the courthouse. So I was wondering, is there anyone you could call over or visit until I'm done?"

Alyssa was caught off guard by that.

"Is it necessary to keep watching me?" she asked. It sounded more blunt than she meant it to. The man didn't seem perturbed by it.

"I think we'd all feel better about leaving you alone once we figure out who put that bomb in your car," he answered. "Fake or not, it took a lot of effort."

"Not to mention it was creepy."

"That too. So, until the trial, is there somewhere else you can stay? I would offer up a deputy, but the department is spread a little thin at the moment because of another investigation." His expression hardened a fraction. "And I don't know anyone I can trust in the police department."

He didn't trust them? To do what? Look after her?

Why did he care so much? Was this just part of the job?

Calm down, Alyssa, she thought. *He's just being polite.*

"I'm sure Robbie and Eleanor wouldn't mind if I stayed with them for the morning. I could ride with them to the trial too."

Caleb nodded. He looked relieved.

"Do I have time to grab a quick shower first?" Alyssa was suddenly hyperaware of how crazy she must look.

"Yeah, that's fine. I'll wait outside."

"Do you have time to eat with me?" she asked on impulse. That heat—a heat she was starting to associate to the man and no one else—pushed up her neck and into her cheeks at lightning speed. "I mean, we have a lot of leftovers from last night and I think I even have some cereal and, of course, some coffee."

Caleb raised his hand and shook it.

"Not today," he said, voice hard. "I'll be out in the car."

There it was again. One second the deputy showed her compassion and humor, and the next, walls were up and he detached.

What happened to him to make him that way? she wondered.

Or was it just her that turned him off?

"He either had an affair with a married woman, killed a man in cold blood or stole drugs from the police department's evidence lockers." Alyssa looked up from her email filled with work orders. Eleanor sat across from her at the table, sipping her coffee. She shrugged and continued. "Those are the three most popular reasons for why Deputy Foster was transferred to the sheriff's department."

Alyssa felt her eyebrow rise.

"Most popular reasons according to the gossip mill?" she guessed.

Eleanor nodded.

"You have to love small towns and their gossip mills." Alyssa was all sarcasm. Said man had put her into a weird mood. Unlike the day before, they had driven in silence to the Rickmans'. It was like that night hadn't happened at all. Any familiarity between them was gone. Still, she had enough humor in her to roll her eyes at what the gossipers of Carpenter had to say about the man.

"I'm just repeating what I heard," Eleanor said.

"You know, a wise woman once told me that gossip might pass the time, but putting any stock in most of it is a waste." Alyssa gave the woman a pointed look.

"Sounds like a smart woman, if you ask me." A sly smile picked up her lips.

"I like to think she is," Alyssa said, unable to keep her frown stationary. "When she isn't listening to gossip, that is."

Eleanor shrugged again. They quieted. It was always a companionable silence. It made Alyssa miss her mother. It had been almost ten years since she passed, and still there were moments when it felt like no time had gone by at all. Alyssa would have to resolve some of the ache of memory by giving Gabby another call after the trial was done.

"You know, there is one piece of gossip I heard that maybe wasn't as much gossip as I would have liked," Eleanor said after a few minutes had stretched quietly between them. She set down her coffee cup. Alyssa already didn't like what she was going to say. The woman was frowning. "No matter what the reason for the deputy coming to town is, everyone seems to be on the same page about his future plan."

Alyssa's stomach did a weird flip.

"And that is?" she asked.

"When he's done here he'll go—"

Eleanor didn't get to finish her thought.

The world exploded around them.

Chapter Ten

The entire house shook. Eleanor's coffee ran off the table, cup overturned. With wide, terrified eyes, both women looked at each other, paralyzed. Somewhere in the distance a woman started to scream.

That shook Alyssa out of her haze. She got up and ran for the front door. It was flung open before she could touch the handle.

Robbie's face was stone.

He didn't meet Alyssa's stare and instead searched over her head. A small look of relief crossed his face as he found his wife. Then he was back to stone.

"Stay here, Eleanor," he said. "Please."

She started to call after him, but Robbie turned around and ran back into the yard. Alyssa followed, nerves twisting up tight. It didn't take long to figure out what the noise had been.

"Oh my God!"

Robbie and Eleanor lived in a bigger neighborhood than Alyssa did. It was more of a community too. The houses were closer, the neighbors were friends—some even family—and there wasn't a time during the day when it was empty of everyone.

The Rickmans' street curved into a half circle where cute brick houses, colorful mailboxes and green, green lawns sat on either side. Those lawns were now dotting with the men and women who were still home on the weekday.

All of them were in various stages of anguish, fear and shock.

And every single one of them was staring at the house near the end of the street.

Or what was left of it.

"Mary, call the police and fire department," Robbie yelled out to the neighbor across the street. Being older than him and his wife didn't stop the woman from whipping back into her house in an instant. Then Robbie was in the street and running.

Toward the house that was currently in flames.

The one that had exploded.

With her nerves tightening to the point of forming one cohesive clump of fear, Alyssa found her leg muscles pushing her to follow him.

The sounds of her heels hitting the street were quickly drowned out by the chaos around them. Neighbors were shouting to one another while a few joined in on the sprint toward the house. Some stayed in the yards, hands over their mouths and tears in their eyes.

"St-stay here," Robbie yelled out after they made it to the front yard. Alyssa was breathing hard, but Robbie was breathing harder. Both had spent a good chunk of the last year rehabilitating from their gun-shot wounds. Robbie's journey had been more difficult.

"No, *you* stay here," Alyssa retorted, adrenaline giving her a strong second wind. She stood tall.

The house was two stories. Or had been. The explosion seemed to have happened on the second floor, and now the yards were covered in brick, wood, glass and debris of what she guessed had been a bedroom or two. Alyssa just hoped whoever owned the house hadn't been in one of those rooms. But a car parked in the driveway didn't give her much hope.

"He's—he's home," Robbie bit out from behind her.

Alyssa didn't wait for permission or for one of the other neighbors running toward the house to brave the house to see if anyone had survived. The fire department was on the other side of town. It would be at least ten minutes before they showed up.

You've been brave before, she thought, bolstering her courage up. *What's one more time?*

The front door's glass had been shattered like the rest of the windows.

"Is anyone in here?" she yelled into the entryway. The roar and crackle of fire made it impossible to pinpoint if anyone was calling back. She stepped through the middle of the broken door. Her heels cracked already broken glass beneath her feet. She slid on a chunk of it as she ran straight into the kitchen.

"Hello?" she yelled, as loud as she could. Smoke was starting to fill up the open-concept floor plan. She wouldn't be able to yell much longer. "Is anyone in here?"

No one responded.

Alyssa put her arm across her nose and mouth and moved deeper into the house. She didn't stop at the stairs. No one was getting up those. Or down.

She hurried to the backside of the house. The smoke moved in faster, became more aggressive. She summoned up her middle school knowledge of when the firefighters had demonstrated what to do if the house was on fire. Obviously, she would have already failed the lesson, since she'd run *into* the house instead of away from it for safety. But as she couldn't leave without checking the rest of the rooms on the first floor, she ducked low.

A small hallway led to two closed doors. Alyssa tapped the doorknob on the first and, when she found it wasn't hot, opened it. The laundry room was empty. A small window over the washer opened up to the backyard. On the other side of the fence was another house. A man and woman stood in it, gaping at the destruction.

Alyssa hoped Mary had called the cavalry in.

She turned tail and moved to the second closed door, also pausing to test the temperature of the doorknob. It was cool to the touch. She put her hand around it, ready to turn, when a god-awful *crack* split through the air.

Over the sound of a house being devoured, Alyssa heard a man's voice boom.

"Get out!"

The entire house seemed to shift above her.

She didn't waste any more time. Flinging the door

open, she was fully planning on using the room's window as her escape when she saw another empty room.

But it wasn't empty.

"Hey!"

The room was used as an office. A large desk and computer were set up on one wall, while a small sofa was against the other. Picture frames covered the walls along with plaques and awards. However, the dog crate that sat in the corner pulled Alyssa's full attention.

A puppy with dark brown fur stood in the middle of the crate, its tiny *yaps* no match for the noise of everything else that was going on. Alyssa never would have heard him from outside.

"I'm coming," Alyssa said, running over to the crate. The puppy was yapping its head off now. She dropped to her knees, broken glass from the window scraping her bare skin, and tried to flip the lock.

It stuck.

Alyssa cursed beneath her breath. The dog kept barking. And then a sound she didn't know how to even describe drowned both of them out.

The walls shook, picture frames clattered to the floor. She whipped her head around to the open door and watched in horror as the wall of the hallway collapsed. Wall and smoke made a cloud that reached into the office like an oversize hand trying its best to grab her.

Alyssa covered her head but kept working on the latch. The sound of yelling filtered in from the broken window. She didn't care.

"Don't worry, pup, I'm not—" She cut herself off with a round of coughing. "Not leaving you."

With one hard tug the latch finally fell free. She opened the door and held her arms open wide. She wasn't about to let the dog run wild. Not when she was sure they were both on borrowed time while still inside.

The puppy stopped its barking and, thankfully, ran right up to her. Alyssa scooped him up, adrenaline surging so she barely felt the glass bite against her skin. He was heavy and would no doubt be a big dog when he grew up. But what about his owner? Alyssa shook her head, trying to ignore the fate of whoever had been on the second story.

Instead she moved to the window and stood back to kick out at the last two jagged pieces clinging to the frame. The dog squirmed as the first shattered. By the time the second fell, he was all-out trying to escape from her hold.

So Alyssa let him.

She tossed him out of the window onto the grass as another wave of coughing racked her body. The movement finally caught the attention of the man and woman she'd seen in the backyard from the laundry room.

The man started to yell and run toward them.

Alyssa didn't have time to wait and see what he was saying. Without an ounce of grace, she clambered out of the window and fell hard against the ground.

"Come on!"

The man was soon at her side. He put his arms under her shoulders and more or less dragged her to his backyard. Alyssa didn't complain. The smoke had finally gotten to her. She didn't stop coughing until she was lying next to a vegetable garden.

"That was stupid of you. You could have been killed," the man said, standing over her. He didn't say it with any real conviction. "But I'm glad you got Sergeant out."

Alyssa was about to ask who Sergeant was when something wet ran across her face. Then it clicked. The puppy's name was Sergeant. She reached out and stroked her new buddy but felt no joy.

She knew *his* name but not his owner's.

"Please tell me—tell me no kids were in there," she managed, trying to keep from falling into another coughing fit.

"No," he said. "No kids. Just Ted."

The man's wife was all-out weeping next to them.

Then Alyssa remembered something Robbie had told her. About who lived down the street from him. Her body went numb.

"Ted Danfield?" she had to ask, even though she already knew.

The man nodded.

"The one and only."

"WHAT ABOUT THE man with the glasses?"

Caleb was looking across the desk at Captain Jones, both men frustrated.

"We already put an all-points bulletin out on him," Jones repeated. "But apart from what you and Miss

Garner described, we don't have much to go on. We don't even know if he's involved, your suspicions aside."

Caleb had opened his mouth to protest that point—the man in the horn-rimmed glasses had spoken to Alyssa and even given her the keys she'd "dropped" before she found the fake bomb—when Jones held up his hand to stop him.

"Listen, I get it," he said, expression softening. But only a fraction. He still in no way had warmed to Caleb. Especially not after he'd disobeyed direct orders. "You like her and want to protect her. Hell, everyone in Carpenter does. But getting emotionally involved is dangerous." Again Caleb started to argue with that point and again the captain held up his hand to stop him. "I've seen that look," he said. "Hell, I've even seen it on our sheriff's face. And I get it. Our job is to protect people, and sometimes those people get under our skin. But you of all people should understand that letting your emotions take over on a case can make everything worse, not better."

Caleb's defense died on his tongue. He felt his jaw harden. The change in demeanor wasn't lost on the captain. He exhaled with a long breath.

"I promise you we will get to the bottom of this," Jones continued when it was clear Caleb wouldn't add in any of his own remarks. "Just try to be patient. We have good men and women out there searching for this man as well as anyone else who might have information. All we can do until then is—"

A knock sounded on the door, interrupting him.

Before he could answer, it opened. Dispatcher Cassie Gates didn't look apologetic in the least.

"We just got several calls in about an explosion in a residential neighborhood," she rushed. Captain Jones and Caleb both shot out of their seats.

"Where?" Caleb asked, heart galloping.

Don't say Dresden Drive, he thought. *Don't say Dresden Drive.*

"Two-eleven Dresden Drive. We've already dispatched fire and rescue."

Caleb's stomach stopped in its descent to the floor.

"Two-eleven?" he repeated. "I dropped Alyssa off at 198 Dresden," he told the captain. "At Robbie Rickman's house."

Jones turned to the dispatcher.

"Do we know who lives at 211?"

Cassie nodded. Her face pinched in worry. He already didn't like her answer.

"Ted Danfield."

Caleb's mind raced.

"And they said there was an explosion?" Jones asked. "Not just a fire?"

"Yes, sir. All callers said the same thing. They heard a loud *boom* and when they went outside they saw Mr. Danfield's house on fire."

The captain swore.

"Ted is one of the witnesses for the Storm Chasers trial," she added, just in case they hadn't made the connection. But Caleb had. In fact, he'd made one more.

"This morning Alyssa was taken off the witness list because of the *fake* bomb," he said. "So not only is he a witness, Ted Danfield is the *first* witness."

Chapter Eleven

"She what?"

Caleb was about to blow a gasket. He'd kept the gas pedal pressed to the floorboard all the way from the department right up to Robbie and Eleanor's driveway. The rest of the street was filled with fire trucks and rescue workers frantically trying to save at least some of Ted's house plus the two neighboring houses that were close enough that the fire was threatening to spread. Caleb and Eleanor were standing in her front yard. Alone.

"She ran with Robbie toward Ted's," she repeated. "I haven't seen either of them since."

Caleb hated to admit it, but since hearing that it wasn't the Rickmans' house that had been affected, he'd felt nothing but relief. And while half of the department rushed over to Dresden Drive, Caleb had done it with only one person in mind.

And she had run *toward* the explosion.

"Stay here," he told Eleanor. "And when I mean here, I mean don't go back inside, okay?"

Eleanor wasn't a dumb woman.

"In case there's a bomb," she supplied.

He hated to do it, but he nodded. "I don't know if that's what happened to Ted, but I wouldn't take any chances."

Eleanor took a long, ragged breath but nodded.

"Go make sure they're okay," she said.

He didn't have to be told twice.

Deputies and police officers alike were trying to secure a perimeter while the firefighters did their job. Smoke was clouding half of the street. Caleb felt like he was navigating a disaster zone, weaving in between residents and responders alike, trying to find two people among a sea of strangers.

The captain's words of wisdom from earlier seemed like a lifetime ago.

Don't get too emotionally attached. That wasn't just a good rule, that was *his* rule.

Yet here he was, mentally holding his breath until he saw her.

"Caleb!"

He swung around so fast his shoes scraped.

Robbie and a man he didn't recognize were standing on the lawn across from Ted's house. The man's face was ashen. Alyssa wasn't with them.

Caleb ran over to him. "Where is she?"

Robbie held up his hands.

"She's okay," he assured him. "But she's being seen to."

He pointed to one of the ambulances farther up the street.

That breath of relief hadn't released yet.

Instead of getting an explanation, Caleb was running again. He rounded the side of the ambulance, fists clenched, until finally he saw her. "Alyssa!"

Sitting on the tail of the ambulance door, Alyssa looked worse than she had when he'd pulled her from her car the day before. Once again she was wearing a blouse tucked into a nice skirt and a pair of heels, no doubt for the trial, but this time they were wrinkled and covered in soot. Across her knees and shins was blood. Her hair was disheveled and a smear of blackness bridged over her nose and to her chin.

What was perhaps the most surprising part was the puppy sitting on her lap, wrapped in her arms.

It was the only thing that stopped his impulse to wrap *his* arms around *her*.

That breath of relief finally released. It transformed into one question.

"You ran *toward* the fire?"

Alyssa averted her eyes.

Guilty.

So guilty, in fact, that Caleb took a second to really look at her again. "Alyssa, did you go *into the house*?"

She brought her baby blues up to his stare before cutting them away to the dog in her arms. The pup was panting, unaware of his anger.

Not at Alyssa, but at himself.

He should have been with her.

Caleb threw his hands up and walked around the side of the ambulance out of her view. He watched as firefighters made headway on killing the flames. It sobered him.

He walked back around to face the woman. When he spoke his voice was lighter, calmer. "Are you okay?"

Once again he looked at the blood on her legs. There wasn't a lot, but it was still more than there should have been.

"Yeah, I wasn't in the part of the house that collapsed," she said.

Caleb felt his eyes widen. It prompted her to explain her statement. "I was in the back of the house getting him out of his dog crate when that happened. Then we got out through the window. I promise I'm okay."

Caleb focused on the dog. He realized that it wasn't just sitting on her lap. She was holding him to her. It softened his anger at her for being so reckless. She'd risked her life to save a dog. Somehow, though, that didn't surprise him. It was becoming clear that Alyssa Garner had a penchant for trying to save people, dogs apparently included.

"Did they tell you who lives here?" she asked, motioning to the house.

Caleb nodded.

Alyssa's chin shook slightly as she spoke again. "Robbie said a firefighter told him they couldn't ID him for sure but they found a body. Ted lost his wife a few years back and never remarried. They never had kids either, so it's probably a safe bet that it's him." She cleared her throat and started to pet the dog absently. "So what happens now? Surely it's not a coincidence, what happened to Ted and what happened yesterday."

"No, I don't think it was a coincidence either," he agreed. He moved closer so only she would hear him.

The EMT was a few steps away talking to another deputy. "I think someone might be targeting the witnesses from the trial."

Alyssa sat up straighter. "But why did I get a fake bomb that played music and Ted…" She let her words trail off. The smoke in the air around them was reminder enough that Ted had indeed gotten a different surprise than she had.

"I don't know," Caleb answered honestly. "But I intend to find out."

THE TRIAL WAS postponed for two months. Alyssa didn't know the reasoning behind the new time frame, but she did know it meant that the two Storm Chasers were being sent back to their respective prisons. Meanwhile their victims were scrambling to make sense of their new possible reality of being targets, yet again.

"I was supposed to take the stand first," Alyssa had explained to Captain Jones after the fire was officially put out. "Ted is—*was* second. Davis Palmer, one of the managers, was third, and Missy Grayson, one of the bank tellers, was fourth. Then one of the bank-goers, Margret Smith, and lastly Robbie."

"That's a lot of witnesses," he had remarked.

"No one wanted the possibility of them not spending the rest of their lives in prison," she had pointed out.

Just listing the witnesses, though, had made Alyssa feel like squirming. It didn't feel real. Maybe it had all been some crazy misunderstanding…

But then they confirmed it was Ted who had been killed and that some kind of explosive had done the trick. What was left of the device had gone to a lab while Captain Jones and Police Chief Hawser had met to try to figure out a plan for the witnesses who were left.

Finally, all of their houses were searched by bomb squad. Nothing was found, but that did little to ease their nerves. Missy, especially, wasn't keen on the idea of being under house arrest with a guard. Instead she told the captain in secret where she planned to hide out and then left town with her husband. Margret Smith followed their example and by that night Robbie, Eleanor, Davis and Alyssa were the only ones who opted to stay.

Although the couple tried hard to get Alyssa to leave. While she did the same with them.

"Go stay with Robert," Alyssa had pleaded, standing in the hallway at the department. "He's got that cabin on his property you two could lie low in."

Robbie shook his head. "If someone really wants to try to blow us to smithereens, then what makes you think they'll stop because we're outside Riker County?"

"That doesn't mean you have to make it *easier* on whoever is doing this by staying," Alyssa bit out.

"You're one to talk," Caleb said at her shoulder. His sudden appearance made her jump.

"But I've already been targeted," she pointed out, annoyed. "Robbie hasn't yet."

Eleanor reached for her hand.

"We aren't leaving our home," she said calmly. "And we aren't potentially putting Robert or any of our kids in danger by hiding with them." She squeezed Alyssa's hand but turned her gaze to Caleb. "We trust that the men and women of the Riker County Sheriff's Department will figure this all out and, in the meantime, keep us safe."

Caleb gave one curt nod.

Though Alyssa thought she saw an uncertainty there. Still, she already knew one thing for sure. She trusted Caleb Foster, even if he didn't trust himself.

"You're a stubborn woman," Alyssa said with a sigh.

"Takes one to know one." Eleanor winked and dropped her hand. "Now, Deputy Foster, what happens to our Alyssa when we go home?"

It was a pointed question, reminding everyone that Alyssa was indeed stubborn. They'd spent a good few minutes trying to convince her to stay with them instead of alone at her house. She'd declined. If someone was truly targeting witnesses, then having two in one house might entice their bomber to break order and try to take them all out.

Assuming the bomber wanted her dead. It shouldn't, but it bothered her that she'd gotten a fake bomb. Was it just the bomber's way of being theatrical about the start of what he was about to do to Ted?

Alyssa turned her attention back to the conversation, knowing she wouldn't suss out the motive behind the actions of a cold-blooded murderer standing in the hallway at the sheriff's department.

"Everyone will have a deputy keep watch at their residence. Including Alyssa." A muscle in Caleb's jaw jumped. He angled his body so he was mostly facing her. "Because I haven't been off the clock since yesterday morning, I've been told to take the night off to regroup."

Alyssa tried to rein in the raw panic that tore through her. Caleb might not have saved her from any danger in the past two days, but she was finding it hard to shake the idea that his companionship still helped her. It was one thing to survive an ordeal. It was another to live with it. Caleb had helped with that part during the last two days. She didn't know why, or maybe she did but refused to think about it at length, but the idea that the deputy wasn't being forced to keep guard was more than just a disappointment. It was a fear.

"I've asked Deputy Mills to be assigned to you," Caleb added. "I've been partnered with him since I transferred. He's a good man and a good deputy. He'll make sure you're okay."

Alyssa didn't want to, but she nodded. Summoning up a smile of what she hoped resembled assurance, she skipped her gaze across Caleb and the Rickmans.

"That sounds good to me," she lied. "I just hope he doesn't mind a dog in his car."

They all cut their gaze to Sergeant at her feet. Since Ted didn't have any immediate family, that meant the Lab didn't either. The suggestion had been made to send him to the humane society, but Alyssa couldn't do that. Ted had loved the puppy, and Ted had always been nice to her. Until they could figure out a better forever home for the dog, Alyssa had offered to foster him. For a puppy he was well behaved. Plus, he seemed to have taken a liking to her. Maybe he realized what she'd done to save him or maybe it was more to do with the fact that she'd snuck into the break room at the department and fed him half of a ham sandwich. Either way he was coming home with her.

Eleanor and Robbie took turns hugging Alyssa *and* Caleb, to his obvious surprise, before wishing both of them luck. They were taken home by another longtime sheriff's department deputy who promised their safety with enthusiasm. This left Alyssa and Caleb alone for a moment while Deputy Mills collected his things.

"It's been a crazy two days, huh?" she started, avoiding any and all pleas for him to come back to her house. To what? Eat dinner and watch TV? To play with the dog? To just sit and talk? Or not talk at all? Her face heated. There were bigger things to be concerned about. "Probably didn't think a small town like Carpenter had this kind of upset in us."

Caleb didn't smile. "Nothing about this town is what I expected." His answer was low and charged. With what, Alyssa didn't find out.

"I'm ready," Deputy Mills called from the other end of the hallway.

Alyssa nodded and gave Caleb the smallest of smiles. "Good night, Deputy."

It wasn't until she was halfway down the hall that she heard him respond.

"Good night, Miss Garner."

CALEB MIGHT HAVE gone home, but he had no intention of staying there. He stripped off his uniform, took a fast shower, and then dressed in his jeans and a plain

T-shirt he'd gotten compliments for when he was in Portland. He didn't know why that thought had popped into his head when he made the decision to grab that particular shirt, but then again, maybe he did.

Alyssa Garner.

He even hung back long enough to shave his face clean. Then he was out the door with no intention of coming back until the bomber had been caught. While he had meant what he said about trusting Dante, there was a part of Caleb that he couldn't ignore. It wanted, *needed* to see this through with a front row seat. Not a spot in the balcony.

Plus, what he did on his off time was his own business, right?

Caleb spent the next half hour running around Carpenter until he got what he was looking for. Then he pointed the nose of his car in one direction. By the time he pulled into Alyssa's driveway, it was ten after seven at night.

"I was wondering when you'd show up." Deputy Mills got out of his patrol car and stretched.

Caleb figured Dante might give him some grief when he got there. Instead he rolled his eyes.

"Why don't you get back into your car and focus?" Caleb said with a snort.

Dante laughed but obliged. "I'm not doing it because you told me to, I'm doing it because your lady in there just fed me a good helping of apple pie and I really like her." He stretched one more time and got back into the car. "Just for the record," he called through the open window.

Caleb smirked and gathered the bags from his back seat. It wasn't until he was knocking on the front porch that the idea entered his mind that maybe Alyssa didn't want him there as much as he wanted to be there. He looked down at the bags and thought at the very least he could drop them off. Then maybe park down the street to help keep an eye on the house.

But then Alyssa opened the door and gave him a smile he'd never forget.

"Caleb, what are you doing here?" Her smile dissolved. "Is everything all right?"

"Yeah, everything is all right," he hurried. "I just thought you could use some backup." He shook the bags in his hand. Together they held dog food, a box with a collapsible dog crate and two chew toys in them. He dropped his voice low, serious.

"I also was wondering if you have any more pie."

Chapter Twelve

The pie was gone, the dog crate was assembled and Alyssa was yawning. As much as she wanted to pretend she wasn't tired, the fact of the matter was that the day had drained her. She hadn't had a moment to really sit and process what had happened. Let alone try to recover from it. A feat that was probably impossible. At least, until their mystery bomber was caught.

"Thank you for all of this," she said, stifling another yawn. "I'll pay you back."

Caleb waved his hand through the air.

"Don't worry about it," he said. "You ran into a burning building to save the dog. I think you've done enough for one day."

Alyssa felt her face fall before she saw Caleb's concern cross his expression. "Poor Ted. Do you know he visited me in the hospital a few times after the robbery? We weren't close—none of us really were—but afterward he made an effort to check on me. On Robbie too." A lump started to form in her throat. She swallowed and spoke around it, willing herself not to cry. "I don't know if I ever really told him thank you for that."

They were standing in the kitchen, the breakfast bar between them. Caleb's proximity wasn't helping Alyssa to control her swerving emotions. She wanted to let her grief and fear out, but her self-preservation was making a stand. Though one look at Caleb, watching her intently, and she felt every part of her waver.

Even more so when he moved around the counter and put a hand on her arm. "I'm sure he knew you appreciated it."

Alyssa was so surprised by the contact she didn't immediately respond. The heat from Caleb's hand wasn't just pressed against her skin—it felt like it was consuming it. The urge to press more of him against her flew through her mind.

"Thank you," she finally managed, breathy even by her ears.

Caleb didn't smile, but he didn't frown either. An in-between look born of thoughts she couldn't guess at. He dropped his hand and took a step back.

"I'm going to go out to the car now," he said. "I'll help Dante keep watch on the place."

"But you're off duty, I thought."

"True, but sometimes the job doesn't end after a shift." He cracked a quick smile and headed for the hallway.

"Or you could stay here," Alyssa hurried. "I mean, in the house. If you're off duty but still going to work, at least do it in comfort." Her cheeks were on fire. Still she kept on. "And it's not like you haven't done it before, right? Plus, it'll be nice to know I'm not alone."

She was telling the truth, despite the embarrassment pooling in her cheeks. It would have been nice to have anyone like Eleanor and Robbie in the house or her sister or even Deputy Mills. But if *Caleb* stayed?

Well, that would be different. It would *feel* different.

Too bad she wouldn't find out this time around.

"You're not alone," he said. "I— *We* will be right outside."

Alyssa was sure she turned as red as a stop sign, but thankfully her head dipped low and she nodded on autopilot.

"You're right," she said. "Thanks again."

Caleb opened his mouth and then instantly closed it. Whatever he was going to say, he must have decided it wasn't worth saying.

"So, you got a girl back in Portland?"

Caleb was sitting shotgun in Dante's patrol car, and while they'd been shooting the breeze for almost two hours, he hadn't expected that question.

"That's one hell of a segue from talking about sports cars," Caleb pointed out.

Dante laughed. "Not when you keep looking over at the house with this expression."

Dante twisted his face into a comical version of what Caleb assumed was the deputy's attempt at trying to look "longingly" at something. Which he was not doing.

"First off, I'm doing my job by watching the house," he said. "To do that I have to, you know, *look* at the house."

"I'm looking at the house too, but not like that."

Dante attached another mock expression to the end of his words. "I have to figure, if you're looking at her *house* like that, then you must look at the woman inside it with a little more intensity." He shrugged. "And if that's true, I have to also figure you don't already have a girl. Or, if you do, then maybe you shouldn't be paying as much attention to Miss Garner as you are, huh?"

Caleb didn't like the man prying into his personal life, especially in the romance department. But he really didn't like the insinuation that he was wronging another woman by being around Alyssa. He might be prickly but he was loyal.

"Not that it's any of your business, but no, I don't have a 'girl back in Portland,'" he answered, heavy on the air quotes.

Dante snorted. "Hey, now, buddy. Remember, you're the one who wanted to sit out here with me and not in your own car. Don't be surprised if I ask a personal question or two."

Caleb rolled his eyes but knew the man was right. While he could have watched the house from his car, he hadn't wanted to be alone. And he had been truthful when he told Alyssa earlier that he thought Dante was a good man. He sighed and tried to adjust his attitude. "My sister, Kathy, likes to say the chip on my shoulder takes up too much room and no woman can get close enough to me to see that I'm not a 'complete jerk.'"

Dante was laughing again. Caleb couldn't help cracking a grin thinking about his older sister. Even if she did give him grief.

"Sounds like a woman I'd like to meet. Not afraid to call out the hard-nosed Caleb Foster."

Caleb kept his grin wide.

"She's definitely not afraid to try to tango with me," he agreed. Then something happened Caleb hadn't counted on. He kept talking. "I think she'd like Alyssa, though."

This time Dante didn't laugh.

"They broke the mold when they made her, all right," Dante agreed. "Not many people would have done what she's done in the last year *and* the last few days."

They lapsed into an agreeable silence. Then Caleb did something else he hadn't betted on doing. He asked a question he shouldn't have. "So, do you know if she's seeing anyone?"

Dante's face had lit up on his preparing to rib Caleb some more, he was sure, when his cell phone in the cup holder went off. With one look at the caller ID, any hint of humor was wiped clean from the deputy's expression.

"Mills here," he answered, tone hardened. It put Caleb on edge.

Whoever was on the other side of the phone started to talk fast. Caleb couldn't make out the topic of conversation, but the way Dante's body tensed, he doubted he'd like it.

"Yes, sir, I'm here," Dante continued. "Deputy Foster is with me." The other man said something else and ended the call before Dante could say goodbye.

"What's up?" Caleb *really* wasn't going to like the answer. He knew it in his bones.

Dante's hand flitted to his holstered gun.

"Anna Kim, the female gunwoman from the bank robbery, was just found dead along with her prisoner transport," he said, his voice grave.

Caleb's adrenaline spiked. "Was Dupree Slater with her?"

Dante shook his head. "He was on a separate transport. One that was just found back in town. All the guards were dead in the back."

"And Dupree?"

Dante shook his head again, this time with feeling. "Gone."

Caleb swore something fierce.

"I have to check on Alyssa," he said, already opening the car door. "I don't know how he's connected to what's been going on, but I do know that he's already tried to kill her before."

"Caleb," Dante said hurriedly, catching his arm to stop him.

"What?" he snapped back. He was seeing red. Red for a violent, bloodthirsty man who might or might not be coming for the witnesses.

"Get your gun," Dante ordered. "The transport was just found, but it's been out of commission since this afternoon."

Caleb's blood went cold.

"He doesn't just have minutes on us," Caleb started.

"He has hours on us," Dante finished.

Caleb reached for his gun in a holster on his hip.

He'd never put too much stock in ESP or the illogical claim that sometimes you just know something is going to happen, but right then and there, Caleb felt it.

Something bad was about to happen.

"So if he was coming for Alyssa," he said, pulling his gun out and checking it, "then he could already be here."

FALLING ASLEEP WAS EASY. Staying asleep wasn't.

Alyssa wondered if it was a nightmare that had woken her. She'd already been pulled from sleep once by one filled with fire and smoke. It had spread a cold sweat across her body so badly she'd gotten frustrated and changed into the closest thing she could find: an oversize T-shirt she'd caught from a T-shirt cannon at a local football game and a pair of lacy sleep shorts in blue that couldn't be seen, hidden beneath the shirt. Normally she would have worried about the amount of leg she was showing, but then again, the only person she'd invited to stay the night had turned her down.

Alyssa sighed and rolled over. She reached for her glasses, ready to brood at her cell phone. It was only ten o'clock, yet she felt like it should have been way past midnight, creeping up on a new morning filled with the unknown.

Why had the bomber not killed her?

Why was he targeting witnesses in the first place?

What about the man in glasses?

Caleb had assured her he was still being hunted, but they were having no luck. Then again, they hadn't found a few of the courthouse-goers from the morning of the trial. Carpenter might have been small, but it was still big enough to get lost in sometimes.

Especially if that someone *wanted* to be lost.

Alyssa sighed again into the darkness of the room. The sound of stirring made her freeze. She glanced at the corner. The dog crate had been too bulky to place in the master bedroom, but then once Sergeant had gone to sleep she'd felt bad about leaving him alone. She'd snuck into the guest bedroom to sleep near him for comfort. After the nightmare, she realized maybe it hadn't been all about making the dog feel safer.

Either way, there she was, staring into the darkness and trying to push all thoughts of Caleb, the bomber and being afraid from her mind, when she heard it.

The creak.

If she had been in any other house, she might have dismissed it, but she *knew* that creak.

It was the third-step creak. The one that, regardless of a person's weight, still whined at any pressure applied to it.

The image of Caleb creeping up the stairs flashed through her mind. She couldn't deny it created a sense of excitement in her too. Late night, just the two of them, wearing what she was. Had he come to say he wanted to be closer to her? For her safety or for more?

Fantasies she hadn't thought were there before started to move through her thoughts. She sat up and swung her legs over the side of the bed. Her cheeks were already heating up. What would she say? What would she do? What—

A dull *thud* came from her bedroom.

In the opposite direction of the creak.

One unknown sound might account for the deputy, but two?

Alyssa got out of the bed, put her slippers on and tiptoed to the wall. All the lights were off—the only way to get Sergeant to sleep—but she knew the room well enough to move toward the door in the dark without a sound, unlike whoever else was moving through her house.

She hesitated in the open doorway, the hallway night-light giving out only the faintest of illumination. Her sister had teased her about that small light, set on a timer, pointing out she wasn't a little girl. But now, trying to figure out if she was just paranoid and hearing things or if she was stuck between two people creeping around her house, she had never been more thankful for such a small material object. Ducking low, she waited to see who would step into the light first, if anyone was there at all.

Alyssa held her breath, waiting.

For one moment she believed without a doubt she'd been overreacting. That even her house could still produce noises she wasn't familiar with.

But then the unmistakable sound of footsteps padded toward her, coming from the stairs.

Her lips parted, mind already forming Caleb's name, when the small light showed her something else.

Someone else.

"Hello, Alyssa. It's nice to see you again."

Dupree Slater smiled.

Seeing him was worse than any nightmare she'd had.

Because this time she was awake.

Chapter Thirteen

Alyssa tried to slam the door shut, but the man was faster.

He closed the space between them in a flash, grabbing for her before she could scramble away. The commotion woke Sergeant from his sleep. He began barking as Alyssa began screaming.

"No need to be afraid," Dupree huffed, catching her forearm and turning on the light with the other. Like the man, his hand was large. Overpowering. It wrapped around her like a vise she couldn't escape.

She wanted to laugh at his comment, saying he'd shot her and gunned down two others and she had every right to be afraid of him. She wanted to break free from his grip, get something heavy, and make him feel at the very least an ounce of the pain he had caused her and everyone in the bank that day. She also wanted to grab her cell phone and call the cavalry in, guns blazing and ready to put down a man who seemed untouchable.

But all she could do was continue to scream in terror. She'd spent the last year trying to overcome just the idea of the man. And now here he was, somehow managing to sneak into her house in the middle of the night.

It didn't seem real.

It didn't seem fair.

"You're coming with me," he grunted out, trying to contain her as she threw her body away from him. She tried to become deadweight in his grasp. She didn't want to make anything easier on the man. "Whether you like it or—"

Something slammed into Dupree's back so hard it caused his hold on her to break. However, the momentum of the hit sent both of them to the floor. Alyssa scurried backward until her back hit her nightstand. The lamp on it clattered to the floor just as she realized what had helped her escape Dupree's grip.

"Caleb!"

Caleb Foster, in all his beautiful glory, picked himself up and readied to take her nightmare head-on.

"Run," he managed to yell before Dupree was on his feet and in his face.

Alyssa didn't have time to examine the situation any closer. Caleb grabbed the front of Dupree's shirt and threw his weight into him again, hard. Together they went into the wall.

"Go—now!"

Alyssa didn't want to leave Caleb alone with a man like Dupree. She'd seen the evil that he created—lived through it too. She didn't want that for Caleb. She wanted to help the deputy to subdue and stop him, as a team.

"I'll still get her," Dupree growled. It was an awful sound, but it did the trick.

Thoughts of helping flew out of her mind. She got to her feet and ran for everything she was worth.

All Alyssa wanted to do in that moment was listen to Caleb and make sure Dupree never touched her again.

THE MAN WAS TALLER, more muscled, and had already found his second wind. However, Caleb had two things on him.

He put his arm up to block a punch Dupree threw and swung hard with a right cross. It connected with the man and he staggered. Angered, Dupree kicked out and flailed in his direction. Both moves Caleb avoided.

For one, Caleb had more discipline. He waited for an opening and took it, sending his fist into his chest, making Dupree wheeze. It didn't matter how big or bad your opponent was, if he didn't have patience he wasn't disciplined. In Caleb's career he had seen up close what happened to those without discipline in a fight.

They'd lost.

Caleb used Dupree's hesitation while he caught his breath to create more space between them so he could grab for his gun. He'd only holstered it for fear that he'd hit Alyssa in the scuffle. He was sure Dupree wasn't above using her as a last-second shield. Now that she was gone, though, Caleb could do some damage. He pulled out his service weapon, but before he could pull the trigger, Dupree recovered and sent him barreling back into the wall.

A *crack* sounded as the drywall broke against Caleb's back. The air was knocked clear out of him and his gun shot out from his grip away from both men. Dupree used his free hand and brought it up to his neck. It was such a sudden move that Caleb had to bring both of his hands up to keep the man from choking him. He was surprised at how strong Dupree's grip was.

"You think after everything I've been through *you* are going to stop me?" Dupree's voice had lowered to a dark, almost tangible level. Caleb peeled off his hand, but his focus faltered in doing so. Dupree delivered a knee to the groin so severe that Caleb knew he wouldn't be able to stand. He stepped away as Caleb fell to his knees, the pain nearly blinding him.

"I waited an entire year in prison for this," Dupree seethed, taking the moment to gain his own breath back. Blood dripped down his nose and fell to the carpet. He swiped at it. "And if taking her is all I have to do to finish what I started, well, then, *Deputy*, you aren't going to stop me now. No one is."

Dupree staggered toward the door to leave. Or so Caleb thought. For the first time he saw a gun, discarded near the opening. It must have fallen from Dupree's possession in the scuffle. If Dupree got the gun, Caleb had no doubt that the man would kill him. He'd already killed two guards from his transport and most likely the two guards from his partner's. Not to mention the female robber herself.

Then, once he had killed Caleb, he would find Dante, if he hadn't done so already—they had split up to search, but the deputy shouldn't have been too far behind—and then shoot him too. And if Dante couldn't best him, that left Dupree Slater to go after Alyssa.

Caleb swallowed his pain and got to his feet.

Because while Dupree had height, width and violence on his side, Caleb had something better than just discipline on his.

He had someone to fight for.

Caleb charged across the room and once again slammed into Dupree. Together they staggered out into the hallway. This time they didn't hit the floor. Dupree used the wall to keep from falling and turned with a fist ready. Caleb had one too. Neither avoided the other's attack. Pain burst bright in Caleb's right eye while Dupree made his own grunt of pain as he took a fast one to the nose. The blood already there wet Caleb's fist, but he didn't stop. Bringing his other fist around, he drilled it into the man's stomach.

Dupree lost his breath for the second time. In that moment, even in the poor hallway light, his eyes found Caleb's. Rage. Pure and simple rage. Dupree let out a thundering yell and threw his elbow so it caught Caleb against the eye that had managed to avoid all punches so far. More pain lit up his face as he stumbled backward, trying to keep from falling.

"You won't—won't stop me," Dupree said, anger funneling from his mouth and into his words, seemingly strengthening his will to take a beating and then dole one out. "He wants her, he gets her."

That surprised Caleb.

"Who wants her?" he couldn't help asking. He had

put a few steps of distance between them, and now he needed a few seconds to right himself.

Dupree busted out a grin that was chilling. "What? You thought you were the only one sweet on her, Deputy?"

Caleb laughed for the sake of being more dramatic. It sounded hollow, mechanical almost. Definitely not a sound the man was used to making.

"Don't look so worried. Norman's been waiting for her for so long. He will treat her nice."

Caleb wanted to ask who Norman was and why he wanted Alyssa, but the way Dupree had said the word *nice* had put straight fire into his bones.

"No one is taking Alyssa," he seethed, a mile past defensive. A familiar anger was building within him. Last time it had consumed him and destroyed his career. His life. And now?

Now he was going to let it destroy again. And this time he wouldn't be looking for redemption for it.

He had to keep her safe at all costs.

He *had* to.

With all the silent fury created by the senseless death and violence Dupree had been responsible for, Caleb closed the space between them with a kick. It was short but not sweet, connecting with Dupree's abdomen with such force it laid the man out.

Right down the stairs.

He rolled and clattered in a heap of flailing limbs, trying to stop himself until he went stationary at the bottom. Caleb flipped the lights on, hoping to see a man so broken that he wouldn't attempt to prolong their fight. That he'd be finished with trying to resist capture. A man realizing he'd reached the end of the road and would finally, *finally* pay for everything he'd done.

Instead he saw a man sitting motionless.

And then, slowly, start to get to his feet.

"Don't you ever—" Caleb stopped midsentence as Dupree produced a gun from his waistband. There was no hesitation on his part as he pulled the trigger.

ALYSSA'S FEAR PUSHED her legs harder than they'd ever been pushed. She didn't just leave the upstairs, she left her house altogether. Later she'd wonder if her feet even touched the sidewalk as she ran full tilt toward Deputy Mills's patrol car out front. It felt like some kind of dream. No. It felt like a nightmare.

Her body was shaking, her breathing was erratic and her heart was surely about to tear itself from her chest. The situation wasn't improved by the fact that Dante was missing.

Where did he go? Was he helping Caleb?

She fumbled for the door handle, ready to attempt to use the radio to call for help, but the door didn't budge. None of them did.

Alyssa knew the Rogerses next door weren't home and didn't even bother to try her other neighbor, an older woman with a bad hip, to see if she could help. Panic was king. It ruled over her mind and replaced all rational thought with the basic need to survive kicking in. She turned tail and ran across the street to a two-acre lot covered in trees.

I'll hide in there, she thought, pain buoying up from

her feet as she picked up speed. *Caleb will find me. He'll find me and we can—*

"Alyssa!"

Alyssa skidded to a halt next to the curb. She spun around, ready to ask Caleb if he was okay. Her question died on her tongue. It wasn't Caleb standing in her driveway.

"You," she exclaimed, confused. "Why are you here?"

The man wearing horn-rimmed glasses from the courthouse smiled.

"I was worried," he said, walking into the street. "I needed to make sure you were okay."

Alyssa started to back away. She didn't have to understand the entire story to know the man was someone else she needed to run from. Without asking any more questions, she turned once again and ran for the trees.

"Don't run from me," he yelled after her. A moment later footsteps sounded behind her. "I'm not going to hurt you!"

Even over the sound of her fear and panic, Alyssa heard the certainty in his words. It almost made her falter in her escape.

Was she missing something?

Was the man in the horn-rimmed glasses there to help them?

To help her?

An explosion behind her shattered her concentration. Another one followed.

Her body tried to keep running while her head turned so she could look back at the house. Before she could understand anything, her feet tucked under each other. She pitched forward. There was no stopping the impact. She let out a scream as her body crashed to the ground. A beat later and her head whiplashed against the grass.

Pain and nausea paraded to the forefront of her senses and began to cloud her vision.

Those aren't explosions, she thought, mind fogging so fast she didn't have time to fear the man chasing her. Instead darkness swam up, took her hand and dragged her down into the depths of unconsciousness.

But not before she finished her thought.

Those are gunshots.

Chapter Fourteen

Caleb dove backward and missed the bullet by inches. He got to his feet but stayed low as another gunshot cracked through the air. Dupree couldn't see him from his place at the bottom of the stairs, and Caleb wanted to keep it that way. At least until he could put his hands on his own gun.

He kept low and went into the guest bedroom. Sergeant was all-out howling from his crate. Caleb wished he could calm the pup down. Instead he picked up his gun and prepared to enter a firefight. To stop the evil that was Dupree in his tracks. He held his Glock up and out. Steady and ready. Taking a deep breath, he went back into the hallway.

No sound floated up the stairs. Had Dupree been hurt worse than he thought, or was he just waiting Caleb out?

Either way, Caleb was about to find the answer.

He aimed downward and moved into position to get the man at the bottom.

But he wasn't there.

"Dammit," Caleb said beneath his breath. He pulled his gun high again and descended the stairs.

The bottom floor was mostly dark. Alyssa had left the porch light on when she went to bed, and it alone tried to illuminate as much of the entryway as it could. It was enough to see blood on the tile but not the man who had left it.

Where had Dupree gone?

Where had Alyssa?

Caleb moved through the entryway and into the living room. He kept the lights off, his eyes adjusting to the darkness. From there he went to the kitchen.

He cursed below his breath again. The back door was open.

Dupree might have been hurt, but that didn't mean he was slow.

Caleb went down the back porch and scanned the backyard for the man. No one shot toward him, let alone moved. He kept his gaze sweeping as he rounded the side of the house. Despite the noise of gunshots, the night stayed quiet. No neighbors yelling or sirens blaring. Normally that was a good thing.

But for Caleb all it did was highlight the fact that he didn't know where Dupree, Alyssa or Dante was. It was amazing how quickly he'd lost control of the situation.

He should have stayed with her.

Why hadn't he?

Just because he was inside the house didn't mean anything other than he wanted to keep her safe.

But he'd been afraid of exactly what had happened.

Afraid he'd lose control of the situation.

For someone trying to keep from emotions getting

the better of him, he sure had let fear do a number on him.

He should have stayed with her.

The outline of a body pulled his attention toward the front corner of the house. Caleb focused his gun on the man.

"Don't move," he warned. However, the man wasn't moving. He wasn't Dupree either.

Dante's face was bloody. His eyes were closed. The gun in his holster was gone along with his cuffs. Even the radio was missing.

Caleb didn't lower his gun for fear that Dupree was near. He crouched to check for a pulse. He let out a sigh of relief as a beat pushed against his skin. It was shallow, but it was there. Feeling inside the man's pocket, Caleb was happy again for the keys the deputy had kept on him. Hopefully it meant the car was still out front. Caleb left his side to peer around the corner and confirmed the car was indeed still there.

After a quick scan for Dupree came up empty, Caleb ducked and ran for the patrol car. When no one shot at him he unlocked it and reached for a radio. He was quick to call in that a deputy was hurt and Dupree Slater was on the move. It wasn't until he put the radio down, ready to continue the search, that he noticed one detail that put ice in his stomach.

In the lot across from him, right before the tree line started, was one blue slipper, all on its own.

ALYSSA WAS LYING down when she woke up.

Had it all been a dream? she wondered.

But then the blanket of unconsciousness lifted completely, ushering in a wave of pain. It thudded along the back of her head all the way to the roots of her teeth.

Then she remembered she'd fallen and hit her head.

And then she remembered the man in the horn-rimmed glasses.

Alyssa slowly focused on her surroundings, knowing full well she wasn't in her room anymore based on the smell alone. It was a heavy musk with mildew swirled in. *Old.*

The room was dark but not to the point she couldn't see. A fluorescent light on its last legs cupped the middle of a popcorn ceiling and showed a small, faded room. Its one window was boarded up. That alone might have terrified her, but coupled with the man sitting in a corner opposite her, and her heartbeat began to pick up speed. The new surge of adrenaline made the pain in her head worsen.

Apparently it showed.

"You wouldn't have hurt your head if you hadn't run from me," he greeted. "I told you I wasn't going to hurt you, didn't I? So why did you run, Alyssa?"

The man leaned forward and put his elbows on his knees, further showing his disappointment.

And that was what it was. *Disappointment.*

Alyssa might have been confused and scared, but she read that feeling in his body language and expression as clear as day.

But who was he to be disappointed in her?

Also, *who was he*?

"You can talk to me, Alyssa," he continued in her

silence. "You're safe here. So, please, feel free to say anyth—"

"Who are you?" she interrupted. "And where have you taken me?"

The man, who she placed in his thirties if not early forties, let his words hang unsaid for the moment before his smile widened. Had they been in any other setting, maybe a picnic at the park with friends or at a neighborhood barbecue, that smile would have been pleasant. Comforting and friendly. However, in the outskirts of the fluorescent lighting in the beginnings of the shadows of the room, the simple showing of mirth was downright chilling.

"You're a smart woman, Alyssa," he said. "So I won't go along with you being coy on your first question, but I will help you with the second." Before she could ask what he meant by her being coy, the man motioned to the room around them. "We needed to make a pit stop before we went home. I have some business I need to finish, and this place is safe for us until I can do that."

He got up from his chair and walked over to the couch she was on. Alyssa scrambled to sit up. The movement made the pain in her head swim.

"Try not to hurt yourself any more than you already have," the man chided. He took a seat next to her. "Here, let me look at that."

Alyssa slapped his hand away as he reached out for her.

"I don't know who you are, where we are or why you took me," she said, voice rising despite her fear.

"If you're so concerned for my well-being, then why don't you let me leave?"

A muscle in the man's jaw jumped as his teeth clenched. His smile stayed but hardened, like someone trying their hardest to pretend they were still happy with the situation when clearly they weren't. Alyssa instinctively leaned away. If he noticed he didn't show it. Instead he laughed. The sound was forced and bitter.

"I don't know what game you're playing with me, Alyssa," he said, voice eerily calm. "But I don't have the time to join in right now. I'm afraid I have more work to do before we can be together."

Alyssa felt like she was in an episode of *The Twilight Zone*. One where she'd been dropped into a world that looked like hers but was slightly off. The familiarity the man was talking to her with didn't make sense. And definitely not the being together part. She wanted more than anything to point out, again, that she had no idea who he was. Yet her instincts were yelling at her to avoid trying to remind him of that. You couldn't force a person to be stable. Sometimes you just had to try to keep from making him even more unstable.

Still, she had to try to make sense of *something*.

"Work," she said, then paused to clear her throat. It was hard to suppress her nerves. "What work are you talking about?"

The tightness around his mouth smoothed. She'd made the right call not to question his identity again.

"I was hoping you'd bring that up," he said, almost excited. "It's been quite the endeavor, but we're finally nearing the finish line. All that's left is one last wahoo. And it's a big one, Alyssa. I think you'll really like how beautiful it all will be. A great finale to a long season." He reached out and took her hand in his. She didn't dare move. "And now that we're finally together, it will be even better."

Alyssa felt her eyes widen. This man wasn't giving her anything more than vagueness and a creep factor that was off the charts. No recognition flared when she looked into his eyes. At least not before the courthouse parking lot and not with the same intensity. Yet he seemed so certain that there was a relationship between them.

"The bombs are yours," she guessed, thinking she might get more information if she didn't actually ask questions. "The one in my car and then in Ted's house. I didn't drop my keys, you took them from me at the courthouse and then gave them back when you were done placing it. Then you put one in Ted's house."

He ran his thumb across the top of her hand. It took all of Alyssa's self-control not to pull away or slap him again.

"I wasn't ever going to hurt you," he assured her. "But I couldn't abandon the plan either, not after waiting so long to put it in action. Not after all the planning. Even if I never planned for you." He sighed and then took a moment before continuing. Like some lovesick high schooler. "So I compromised. I knew I could still get everyone's attention by planting a fake one. That way I could keep you safe but still follow the correct order."

"I was the first witness for the trial," she added.

"And Ted was the second." He nodded. Although Alyssa was trying to navigate the obviously unstable mind of the man in front of her, she couldn't help breaking her facade to ask a few of the questions burning in her mind. "But what's the point of all this? Why kill witnesses for the trial? Surely you have to know the Storm Chasers would still be found guilty without us. Why help Dupree and his partner?"

The man used his free hand to pat the top of hers like he was trying to placate a child. "I couldn't care less about the trial. Or the 'Storm Chasers.' My goal is and has always been bigger, the payoff much sweeter. Especially now that we're together again. But don't worry, everything will make sense soon. All you have to do is be patient and stay here, okay?"

Alyssa's focus had stuck on the "together again" portion of his answer. It kept her from responding right away. The man wasn't pleased.

The hand holding hers tightened.

"Okay, Alyssa?" he repeated. His smile skewed, no longer aligned with a pleasant mood. His grip was now tightening past annoying to painful. "You'll stay here, right?"

Tears pricked at the edges of Alyssa's eyes.

She nodded.

"Say it, Alyssa," he demanded, voice cutting low and mean. He added his other hand to the grip and squeezed so hard she couldn't keep from yelping. "Promise me that you'll stay here."

"I promise," she rushed.

"You promise *what*?" The man's intensity tripled. He was yelling now. *"What do you promise, Alyssa?"*

"I promise I'll stay here," she cried. "I promise!"

All at once the man returned to what she could only guess was his normal. He let go of her hand, and his smile brightened.

"Good," he said. "I'd hate to see you lose your way. I know you've been forced to spend some time with Deputy Foster. I'd hate for him to get into your head and mess up everything we have. Everything we could have."

At the mention of Caleb, Alyssa felt herself freeze.

Where was he?

Was he okay?

Looking into the eyes of the man in front of her, she dared not ask him.

He wasn't just a man who was unstable. He was a man filled with delusions. Ones that involved her. And her instincts warned her that if she didn't play along with her part in his daydream, they would come to a deadly end. But she couldn't police the fear that had welled up inside her. It pushed the dam to the point of extreme. The tears she'd been trying to hold back started to roll down her cheeks.

If the man saw them, he didn't seem to care.

"Well, now that we have everything settled, it's time for me to have a talk with an old acquaintance." He leaned forward and pressed his lips against Alyssa's forehead. Every part of her body felt disgust. Thankfully, he stood when he was done. "Don't worry, once this is all over we can have the life we've always wanted."

He left the room and closed the door behind him.
The sound of a dead bolt sliding into place followed.
Alyssa was glad he was gone.
At least now she could cry in peace.

Chapter Fifteen

They all looked like fireflies. Dotting the neighborhood with their flashlights, uniforms converged on Alyssa's property and then expanded out in an attempt to find Dupree and Alyssa. Guns were drawn, shouts were exchanged, neighbors were told to stay indoors, but no one set their eyes on the beautiful auburn-haired woman.

Or the beast who had managed to escape.

Hours crawled by, and with them Caleb's sanity inched further away from him. Dante had been rushed to the hospital and diagnosed with a fractured cheekbone and a nasty concussion. The doctor had refused to let him join the search on the basis of, at the very least, him being medicated out of his mind. His speech was even more impeded by the swelling around his cheek. He'd at least been able to express his guilt and anger at letting Dupree get the jump on him when they split up to check the perimeter after getting the call that he'd escaped.

But Caleb didn't hold it against the man. It had been *his* fault, not Dante's.

That fact kept becoming more pronounced as time slipped by. His darkening mood didn't go unnoticed.

"I order you to go home."

Captain Jones stood to the full of his height and pointed in any direction that was away from the department. With no new evidence, some of the men and women had regrouped for a new game plan.

"I'm not leaving until we find her," Caleb said with a hardness one wouldn't normally use with a superior. He just wanted Jones to know that it was more of a promise than a statement.

Whether the captain understood the tone or not, he also stayed firm in his decision.

"You need to get some rest," he said. "There are plenty of men and women, including the local police department, who are out there searching for both Miss Garner and Dupree." Caleb opened his mouth to protest, but Jones was quick to continue. "The dogs will get here at five and after they are done I will update you. But as of *right now* I am telling you to go home."

"I'm off the clock," Caleb pointed out, anger building inside him. It wasn't aimed at the captain but himself. "You can't order me around now. If I want to keep looking, I will."

Jones's lips narrowed and his nostrils flared. This time his anger *was* directed at Caleb. "This is a stressful situation. Never mind the emotional attachment between you and Miss Garner. So I'm going to give you a pass here and ignore that look and tone you're giving me. You're getting close to crossing that line again, Mr. Foster. Not with just me but the department as a whole.

And that's not something you can afford." He took a noticeably deep breath and then let it out slowly. Like he was trying to calm down. Jones's eyes then dropped to Caleb's hands, now balled into fists, before he spoke again. "Helping people is what we do. Ensuring their safety, even when it means we lose ours. You haven't been here long, so let me make you a promise. The men and women of the Riker County Sheriff's Department are extremely capable, hardworking people. We will always be here for our community and stop at nothing to ensure their well-being."

Jones took a step closer. He lowered his volume. "Trust us and listen to me. Go home. Sleep for a few hours and then get your ass back here. Just don't waste any more of my time having to babysit you. *Go home now.* Or I'll escort you there myself."

The captain didn't budge from his new stance. Caleb didn't have to know the man well to understand exactly what his body language was saying. He meant every word, including the threat, and he wasn't going to back down in the slightest. But he was right, in part. Their conversation alone was wasting time.

Time that could be spent finding Alyssa.

Caleb gritted his teeth and gave Jones a nod. There wasn't any more to be said. The captain stayed still as Caleb turned and left the building. He walked to his car, hands still fisted.

Even if the captain was right, that he needed to trust the rest of the department, it didn't make a dent in his resolve to continue to look on his own. Trust wasn't easy for Caleb. Not after what had happened. Especially not with Alyssa on the line. He couldn't just go home, get into bed and sleep hours away.

No, not when he had no idea what she was dealing with at the moment.

If she was even still al—

Caleb slammed his hands against the steering wheel.

"Don't think like that," he yelled at himself. "She's tough."

He tried to distract his mind from looping back around to the worst possible outcome until he realized he'd disobeyed direct orders once again. He parked his car outside Alyssa's house and sank back in his seat.

Why was he even here?

Two headlights interrupted his thoughts as a pickup truck pulled up beside him. Caleb reached for his gun. It was nearly four in the morning and no one, not even him, had a reason to be there. Caleb readied to pull his gun just in case when the truck's window rolled down. He immediately dropped his hand and let out a breath he hadn't realized he'd been holding. He got out of his car and walked up to the window.

"What are you doing here?"

Robbie was alone in the truck and looked ready. For what, though?

"I've been looking for you," the man said back, hurried. Impatient. The tone put Caleb on alert. "I thought you might be here."

"Why? What's up?"

Robbie's face hardened. "Do you have any leads on Alyssa or Dupree?"

Caleb didn't like to, but he shook his head. "No, everyone is still looking."

"And you?"

"I was told to go home." Caleb motioned back to the house. "But I wound up here."

Robbie lowered his voice.

"Do you have your gun with you?" he asked. It surprised Caleb, but he answered without skipping a beat.

"Yeah, why?"

Robbie leaned out of the window. "Because I think I know where Alyssa might be."

ALYSSA'S FINGERS WERE bloody and her shoulder and head ached.

While her captor was gone she'd spent the last hour trying to actively escape her makeshift prison.

The boards on the window wouldn't budge. They were held together by so many nails that not even one shifted as she pulled with all her might. Not that it would have made much of a difference if she managed to pull one off. Through the gap in the top layer of boards, she saw that on the other side of the glass was another layer. Still, she kept her focus on that window long enough to make her fingers rub raw at the attempt.

Once that route was proven to be a dead end, she'd gotten a little desperate. Trying to pick the lock was impossible thanks to having no tools of any kind, not even a bobby pin, never mind the skills or knowledge to do it. So she'd sucked in a deep breath, pulled herself together and then charged the door like a bull at a red flag. However, the door wasn't as worn as the rest of the room. It creaked but didn't budge. By the third attempt, all she was doing was breaking herself down, not the door. And she wanted to be the best she could be when the man returned.

She took a seat on the couch and tried to focus on anything she could turn into a weapon. Had the man had a gun when he was in the room with her? Alyssa tried to remember, but all thinking about him did was send a chill down her spine.

The way he talked to her.

The way he *looked* at her.

Was she missing something?

Did she know the man?

Footsteps sounded in the hall outside the door. Alyssa scrambled to her feet and looked around one last time in the hope that she'd missed some glaringly obvious pipe or baseball bat or vase—*anything*—but she knew she hadn't. The dead bolt slid open. Maybe if she treated the man like she had treated the door she could buy herself a window of escape.

She readied herself, bending slightly, ready to go, but the door didn't open.

Instead she heard the man from before talking to someone else. She moved a step closer to try to make out what they were saying.

"It's my choice. Not yours." Another chill ran down her spine. That was definitely the man in the horn-rimmed glasses. And he was angry.

"This isn't part of the plan," the second voice said even louder than the first. There was no chill cold or deep enough that could fully express her feelings for that voice. It was Dupree Slater's. "*She* isn't a part of this plan and never was. Get rid of her."

Alyssa took an involuntary step backward.

Her panic levels had been holding steady the last few hours. Now they were increasing at an alarming rate. She almost didn't hear the other man's response.

"There will be *no* plan if you touch her," he yelled, volume going from zero to a hundred in a second flat. Dupree reacted in kind, his voice more an extended boom than words.

"This connection you think you have with her isn't real. *She doesn't remember you.* And do you want to know why?"

Alyssa jumped as the sound of a tussle bled through the door. Muttered cursing followed and then Dupree had the door open. Alyssa let out a shriek as he moved toward her with startling speed. Her back slammed the wall just as he reached for her head. Out of terror she closed her eyes, waiting for what she thought was a punch to her face. Instead something unexpected happened.

She felt her glasses slide through her hair and across her skin. Dupree pulled them off her face and whirled around to the other man. He held her glasses up and shook them. Then he dropped them to the floor.

And stomped on them.

"*This* is why," Dupree bit out.

He walked over to the door and stopped. Alyssa blinked a few times to focus, but he was still a blur.

"How many fingers am I holding up?" he asked.

"Wh-what?"

Of all the things he could have said, that hadn't even made her list of possibilities.

"How many fingers am I holding up?" he repeated, raising his voice.

Alyssa knew that there was no way other than to wear her glasses to answer him correctly. Still, she squinted and tried.

"I'm nothing but a blur, right?" he added.

Alyssa nodded.

What did it matter that she couldn't see?

"That's what I thought." Dupree must have looked at the other man. His tone changed into a smugness that made the situation even more confusing for Alyssa. "She might have looked at you, but she didn't *really* see you. And if she didn't see you, Norman, then how did that connection happen?"

Alyssa didn't understand what was going on, but now at least she had a name to give the man in the horn-rimmed glasses. *Norman.* Though that wasn't the best feeling, considering the name brought her no recognition.

"That's enough," Norman growled. There was undeniable authority thronging through his voice. Dupree had hit a nerve. A big one. "We have work to do."

The blur that was Dupree didn't leave right away. Instead he stood next to Norman with a look Alyssa guessed wasn't polite in the least. Then, without another word, he left them alone.

Alyssa felt her body relax a fraction. While she had no love for Norman, in her book, he was better to be with in close proximity than the man who had shot her the year before. But no sooner than she'd had that thought did it change.

Norman closed the space between them. His face swam into focus when he was an inch or two in front of her nose. He put his hands on the tops of her arms. She couldn't move away. He smiled.

"Don't worry," he whispered. "He just doesn't understand what we have. But you do, don't you?"

Alyssa felt frozen. Not even fear could unthaw her this time to play along with him.

However, Norman didn't seem to care. He kept smiling. "When I found out you had survived… Well, I knew what you gave me was more than a look. It was a promise." He reached up and tucked a strand of hair behind her ear. "One that said we'd be together when all this was over."

He stepped away and blurred.

"And we will," he finished. "Just one last step."

Alyssa's fear gave way long enough to ask one question. "And what *is* that step?"

"Revenge," he said, matter-of-factly. "Sweet, sweet revenge."

Chapter Sixteen

"Are you sure about this?"

Caleb and Robbie were parked at the mouth of a street lined with abandoned houses just outside downtown Carpenter. Two lone streetlights were the only things that seemed to be in order in the one-block stretch. Aside from the electrical buzz, nothing and no one else stirred.

At least not outside.

Robbie rubbed his hands together, tense.

"I don't know how much Alyssa has told you about it, but during our recovery we spent a lot of time together," he started, eyes never leaving the house in the middle of the block. "She's a strong cookie, but anyone in her position would have had a difficult time. And she did. One day her physical therapist suggested she find something else to focus on like reading or a hobby. Basically anything that would help her cope and work through what had happened. So she focused on the one part of her life that she couldn't make sense of."

He nodded in the direction of the houses. "She

couldn't understand why Dupree Slater did what he did. So she spent most of her recovery trying to figure out who he was." He shrugged. "She thought if she knew about his life she could find out how he ticked, and if she knew why he'd shot her, then everything would hurt less."

Caleb felt an ache in his chest. He could imagine Alyssa pretending everything was all right while trying to desperately make sense out of senseless violence. In that way he could relate to her without hesitation. His career—his past—had proven to him that sometimes there just was no answer.

"Did she ever figure it out?" Caleb asked anyway.

Robbie shook his head. "Eventually her sister, Gabby, Eleanor and I sat her down and convinced her that some people are just bad and do bad things and that it was time for her to move on." Robbie gave a small smile. "And she did, but not before she got a little backstory on Dupree." He pointed to the houses. "Or his brother, who lived in town before his house and his neighbors' were abandoned after a fire broke out and made them unlivable. No one had insurance and the city hasn't been able to touch them. That house is the only tie Alyssa ever found between Dupree and Carpenter."

Caleb sat up straighter. "And you wanted to find me and not tell another deputy because…"

"The last time the cops were called in, Dupree killed two people, and almost took another," Robbie answered, solemn. "I figured Alyssa has a chance of living through this if we do it quick and quiet. And try not to anger the beast that is Dupree any more than he already is. There's no telling what he might try to do."

Logically, it might have made more sense to call in backup. More manpower, more coverage. But part of Caleb—the part that cared for Alyssa more than it should have—didn't want to risk a team of people going in either. But he also didn't want to risk Robbie going in too. He had a pretty good suspicion that Alyssa would never forgive him if he let something happen to one part of her favorite couple. And, he had to admit, the old man and his wife had grown on him in the short time since he'd met them.

"Okay, here's the plan," Caleb said, pulling his gun out and checking the chamber. "I need you to do exactly as I say."

THE LIGHTS WENT out right as Norman was leaving the room. It was a nightmare within a nightmare for Alyssa. Now her last hope of seeing anything without her glasses was gone. She hugged the wall as Norman cussed. At least he wasn't as enthusiastic as he had been before.

Footsteps hurried toward their room. A small flashlight bounced down the hallway. By the blur's shape it was easy to guess it was Dupree.

"A truck is parked on the other side of the street," he said, clearly angry. "The security guard from the bank is inside and he's talking on the phone. That can't be a coincidence."

Why was Robbie outside? And just like that, worry clenched her chest. But so did hope. Surely he wouldn't have come alone.

"Don't make a scene," Norman advised. "But take care of it. I'd like to stay under the radar as long as possible."

"So otherwise, be quiet when I kill him," Dupree said.

"You got it."

Alyssa's fear turned a corner and ran smack-dab into anger. Like a bucket of ice water to the face, she felt a jolt. She had to warn Robbie.

"Norman," she called into the darkness after the bounce of Dupree's flashlight retreated away from them. She tried to soften her voice, showing affection. Even if he'd just ordered her friend to be killed.

Norman must not have had a light on him. He answered her in the darkness.

"Don't tell me you're afraid of the dark?" he said. "After everything you've been through already."

For the first time Alyssa heard a Southern drawl.

"I'm afraid of Dupree," she said, voice not as steady as she liked. "I don't trust him." Alyssa took an uncertain step forward. The darkness was near debilitating. But she had to do *something*. "And neither should you. He could—he could hurt you, Norman. He could kill you."

Again Alyssa took a step forward. It was small and her slipper shuffled at the movement. There was no sound in return. Norman must still be in the doorway. Trying to watch her.

"You don't have to worry about that," he said, a degree less harsh than when he'd been speaking to his partner.

"He shot me in the back!" Alyssa's voice broke, but from anger, not pain. "I wasn't a threat and he shot me. What's stopping him from doing it again to both of us?"

This time there was a sound in the darkness as Norman's shoes moved across the floor. Alyssa fought the urge to flinch away from it.

"Dupree helped prove we were meant to be together," he said, getting closer. "When you survived, I knew it was a sign. And for that I'm grateful. But now that I know, *he* knows the limits and he'll respect them." The heat of another body radiated out to her. She felt his breath when he spoke. "As long as you stay by my side, Alyssa, I won't let anyone hurt you." She nearly screamed when his hands grabbed the tops of her arms again, holding her in place.

It made her wonder how he even knew where to grab in the dark. Even if she'd had her glasses on, the boarded-up window didn't allow any outside light in. He should have been as blind as she.

Which gave Alyssa an idea.

One that might possibly have been terrible.

Knowing exactly where his hands were and that

they were occupied, Alyssa took a risk. With all her might she kneed Norman as hard as she could where the sun didn't shine.

His pain was instantaneous. He let go of her arms and wailed. As soon as their connection was broken, Alyssa pushed forward until the man sounded like he'd fallen over. She moved as quickly as if her life depended on it. Which she was sure it did.

Alyssa outstretched her arms until she felt the opened door. Without Norman blocking the entrance she could just make out light in the distance. Which could be Dupree. Either way she had to get out of that room.

Because while Norman had seemed sincere in his words, the only promise of protection she believed in had been from a man named Caleb Foster.

Dupree took the bait.

Caleb watched as the man left through the back door and disappeared around the side of the house. He was cautious, trying to scope out his surroundings to make sure Robbie was alone. And that was exactly what Caleb had wanted him to do.

As soon as Dupree disappeared, he hurried to the back door, clicked on his flashlight and entered the house. While he wanted more than anything to bring a world of justice down on Dupree Slater's head, he had to make sure Alyssa was in the house. If he apprehended the man or had a shoot-out and won and

Alyssa was hidden somewhere else? Well, that wasn't something he wanted.

No. First he had to find her. Then he'd deal with Slater.

Even without the fire and water damage, the house was old. Caleb slightly regretted turning the breaker off. His small beam of light couldn't show him every part of the playing field. He just hoped he wasn't about to step into a hole in the floor.

He had navigated halfway through the house when he finally heard movement. Hope and relief welled up inside him so fast he was seconds away from calling Alyssa's name when those footsteps were coming fast toward him. He moved the beam of light to the source.

"Alyssa?"

Her eyes met his. They were wide, terrified.

"Caleb?"

She collided into his arms, but the embrace lasted only a second. The flashlight beam skittered to the wall. For that one moment there was only the two of them, holding on to each other in the darkness. Then it was gone, and Alyssa was pulling back. Still, it was long enough for Caleb to be surprised at how badly he'd wanted to feel her in his arms.

"We have to hurry," Alyssa rasped. "He's behind me."

"Dupree is outside. I need you to stay here until I can—"

"Norman is the boss," she interrupted. "*He's* behind me."

That new piece of news was followed by the grunting of someone in pain at the end of the hallway. Caleb's plan certainly hadn't accounted for another man. Who was Norman?

"We have to go," Alyssa added, grabbing his hand and tugging. The warmth of her hand put him into gear. He turned around and whispered back to her to keep quiet. The last thing he needed was to be caught between an unknown man and Dupree. Even with a gun, that was one too many variables for his comfort.

Caleb cut his flashlight off and navigated the path back out of the house with relative ease. Dupree hadn't come back, and Norman had started to make more noise. Which meant their window to get away from both men was closing.

"We need to run," he rushed, turning them toward the back fence. If they could get on the other side and keep going, then Robbie could get Alyssa and take her to safety before Dupree realized which direction they'd gone. Then Caleb could fight. He could end this.

Caleb stopped just short of the fence. It was chain link and showed that the backyard of the house next door was just as desolate as the one they were currently in. Alyssa hesitated in front of it.

"Don't worry, I'm here. I have you," Caleb assured her. He moved aside to help her climb the fence, giving her a push up until she was on the other side. He followed, but not before a sound he was hoping not to hear yet rang through the air.

It was a gunshot, but it wasn't directed toward them.

"Go, go, go," Caleb yelled, grabbing Alyssa's hand again.

If he was right, then Dupree had just shot at Robbie. Which meant the distraction had reached its end and soon all hell would break out. Caleb just hoped he could get Alyssa clear beforehand.

They ran around to the corner of the new house, jumped one more fence and then paused in the side yard. It had less damage than the other two on the street but was boarded up tight. They weren't getting inside any time soon if they needed to hide.

"We need to get to the end of the street," Caleb whispered, dropping her hand. "I have to call Robbie."

Alyssa didn't comment. Her breathing was heavy, erratic. Like it had been in the car when she thought the bomb beneath her seat was real. Panic verging on an attack or hyperventilation. Neither ideal for their current situation. Even more of a reason to put urgency into his every action. She knotted her fist on the back of his shirt and followed along without complaint as they hurried into the next house's side yard. He used his free hand to fish out his cell phone and call his now number one contact.

It rang twice, but thankfully Robbie answered.

"Did you find her?" the older man greeted. He too sounded geared up.

"Yeah, and another man," Caleb said, still keeping his voice low. "We're running toward the end of the street, trying to stay out of sight. Pick us up at the corner."

"I don't know if I can," Robbie hurried, adding in a stream of nasty, heated words. "After I drove off, Dupree jumped into a car and peeled out after me. He's on my tail and shooting."

Caleb in turn cursed beneath his breath.

Their backup wasn't able to help them.

"Drive straight to the sheriff's department," Caleb said, waiting for Alyssa to come around him and open the gate to the backyard. "Call them and tell them the situation. Drive smart and fast."

"Keep her safe," Robbie answered.

Caleb ended the call.

"What's happening?" Alyssa's voice had a tremor running through it.

"A change of plans," he answered honestly. "But nothing we can't handle. We just need to put distance between us and them."

Caleb reached for her hand, ready to run, but Alyssa pulled away.

"I—I can't," she whispered. "I—I just can't."

Even in the poor light around them, he could see she was freezing up. It caught him off guard. It was the first time he'd seen such a strong reaction from her. Eyes wide, breathing erratic, lips trembling. She wasn't beginning to panic; she was beginning to lose it.

"You can," he said, squeezing her hand to try to assure her. "All you have to do is hold on to me and I'll get us out of this."

Alyssa shook her head, her blue eyes still wide.

"He broke my glasses," she said, voice going hollow. As if she was trying to distance herself from her fear. "Dupree broke my glasses. And it's dark."

It finally clicked in place. He should have realized she wasn't wearing them. And why she was so terrified. She really couldn't because she was blind without her glasses. The extreme vulnerability now fit. And it made Caleb pause.

An overwhelming wave of feeling surged through him.

Without a second thought he grabbed her chin and angled her face up. Then he met her mouth with his own.

The kiss was meant to distract Alyssa from her fear. To give her something else to focus on. Something, he hoped, that was good. He also hoped it reminded her that he was there. Down in the trenches with her. Not going to move an inch unless she did too. That, no matter what, he'd get her to safety.

Yet all thoughts and intentions fell away as the warmth of her lips pressed against his. Those pink, pink lips aroused something almost primal in him. He wanted it to last. He wanted it to evolve.

He wanted her.

But he had to get her to safety first.

Caleb pulled away, breaking the kiss.

"Listen to me," he said. "You are one of the strongest people I know, and I'm right here with you. Together we can do this. You just have to trust me. Please."

Once again he reached for her hand.

This time she didn't back away.

Instead she slipped her hand in his. "I trust you."

Chapter Seventeen

They made it around another house before their mystery man named Norman started to shout. Caleb didn't like how close his words were. Or the gunshot that exploded in the early morning air right after them.

Caleb yelled out as a searing pain cut through his left arm. He backtracked hard, guiding Alyssa to the side yard of the last house they needed to get on the other side of before they were at the end of the street. Not that he had a great plan for when that happened. He'd been hoping the other man would stay off their trail so Caleb had more time to figure out an escape. Or at least had time to wait out help.

"Were you hit?" Alyssa yelled, clutching his hand.

Before he could answer, another shot sounded. Dupree wouldn't have had the time to double back and be on them. It had to be Norman.

"We need to run around the front while he's shooting over here," he said, already picking up speed. Alyssa didn't argue.

"She's mine," the man yelled. The voice carried to them with an ease it shouldn't have because of their distance. Which meant there wasn't much of it between them anymore. That fact alone tainted their victory of finally getting to the end of the street. Their last obstacle.

"What now?" Alyssa asked, breathless.

The street they were on intersected with one that had seen better days. It led to a network of other neglected streets that dumped into more-used routes. According to Robbie, before the fire that effectively made the houses behind them uninhabitable, the surrounding areas had been more used. But after the fire, a lot of Carpenter had somehow all decided to steer clear for one reason or the other.

So, expecting someone to drive by the exact area they were in, especially so early in the morning, was a very, *very* long shot.

As for hiding until they could call someone in?

A field of green stretched out beyond them on the other side of the street. Trees were in the distance, but there was no way they could make it to them without being exposed for several minutes.

"Alyssa!"

Norman sounded enraged as he yelled her name. Caleb didn't like how close the sound was either. He looked at the house behind them.

"I need you to stay here," he ordered, pointing Alyssa toward a gap between two bushes still miraculously alive against the back end of the house. "Stay low and don't come out until I say."

"But what about you?" she rushed.

It was endearing, he had to admit. Even with some

madman yelling her name and chasing them with a gun, she was still worried about him.

"I'm going to stop this man named Norman," he promised. "Because you are *not* his."

He could tell Alyssa didn't like the idea, her brow drawn in as a look of concern clung to her expression. Still, she did as she was told and crouched down in the gap.

"Be careful," she whispered. "That's an order."

Caleb couldn't help smiling.

"Yes, ma'am."

He pulled his gun high and crept around the front of the house. There was a fifty-fifty chance Norman was making his way toward them through the front yards, while there was also a fifty-fifty chance he was going around the back. Caleb kept his breathing as steady as he could and hoped he'd chosen the right direction.

When he'd planned on going toe-to-toe with the man responsible for taking Alyssa, he'd hoped that he'd have her well hidden or out of danger altogether. And that he'd be dealing with Dupree. Not some mystery man. Now Alyssa was hiding in the bushes while he was making decisions that could easily backfire.

Which was exactly what happened.

No sooner was he aiming his gun out around what used to be the front porch than Alyssa let out a gasp loud enough that it drew his attention backward. Caleb spun around, gun ready, and felt his stomach plummet.

A man was standing next to Alyssa, his own gun pointed at her head. He was panting but in no way looked any less dangerous. And it wasn't just any man.

"You," Caleb bit out. "I knew you had something to do with all this."

The man with horn-rimmed glasses managed a quick grin.

"You really *are* good with faces, but don't feel bad, *Deputy*," Norman said in between catching his breath. "I've fooled smarter people than you."

Norman was a few feet from Alyssa, but that didn't comfort Caleb in the least. Even if the man was a poor shot, the chances of him hitting her if he pulled the trigger were too high.

"What do you want?" Caleb asked, his own gun aimed forward. He could hit Norman if he wanted to, but what if the man pulled the trigger before he could stop him?

There were too many variables.

And none of them were good.

"I want you to leave us alone," Norman practically growled. His demeanor shifted into what Caleb could only describe as disgusted. "Stop trying to save her when she isn't yours to save!" Spit flew out of his mouth as he yelled. His face turned red.

Caleb didn't have time to be confused. His attention listed over Norman's shoulder to a pair of headlights in the distance. Caleb hoped beyond all hope that it wasn't Dupree making his way back.

"You should mind your own business," Norman added, unaware of the car. He shook the gun. Caleb realized it wasn't because he was trying to appear more threatening. Instead it was the man's emotions bleeding through. He was angry.

Really angry.

Reckless.

"You put a bomb in her car," Caleb pointed out, trying to buy time to devise a plan that wouldn't risk Alyssa getting shot or caught in the cross fire. "She needed help, so I helped."

Norman shook his head with fervor.

"It wouldn't have hurt her," he defended. "She didn't need you or your help. She still doesn't. She needs *me*. Not you confusing her."

The car was close enough that Caleb could see it wasn't a car at all but a four-door Bronco.

One he'd seen before.

"Then let her stand up," Caleb said, thinking fast. "You have a weird way of showing you want to protect her if you won't even let her *stand up*."

It was a weird thing to say, he knew, but Caleb hoped it would do the trick.

"Of course she can stand up," Norman answered.

"Then let her!"

Norman's nostrils flared, but he addressed Alyssa directly. "Show him, Alyssa. Stand up!"

Alyssa followed the order without comment. She might have been unable to see the Bronco barreling toward them, but now, Caleb hoped, the driver could see her.

Thankfully, he did.

The driver changed course just in time to jump the curb.

"Run," Caleb yelled.

Alyssa's sight might have been compromised, but

her legs didn't have any trouble moving. Norman whirled around but didn't act like a deer in headlights. What he had in anger he also had in speed. He dove out of the way as the Bronco hit the side of the house, separating Caleb and Alyssa from the rage-filled Norman.

The driver's door swung open, but the man inside didn't make it out before gunshots slammed into the other side.

"Get in," the driver yelled.

Caleb didn't need to be told twice. He ran to Alyssa's side and helped her into the back seat floorboard. When he shut the door he lay on top of her, elbows on either side of her body, shielding her from any bullets that made it through. "We're in!"

Metal scraped against wood as the Bronco floored it in Reverse. Glass shattered overhead.

"Backup's behind me, but we're going to get you two out of here first," the driver yelled. "Hold on!"

Caleb kept his gaze down, eyes only for the woman staring up at him. The motion of going backward shifted his body against hers. It was a welcomed feeling. Concrete proof that she was with him.

"Are you okay?" he asked. The Bronco swerved to the side and then shifted into Drive. "Did he—did they do anything to you?" He moved the hair out of her face, more to check her skin for any signs she'd been touched. It was as clear as it had been the night before.

A wild expression crossed Alyssa's face. It was one Caleb couldn't place. He opened his mouth to repeat his question with more force, already getting angry at the possible answer, but she was faster.

Alyssa threw her arms around his neck, pulled him against her and kissed him hard. Unlike the kiss he'd given her minutes before to help focus her attention, this one was rough and hungry. It pulled his breath from him and begged for more.

And he wanted that.

Parting her lips with his tongue, he finally was able to taste her, returning the kiss with equal force. After days of danger and uncertainty, Caleb answered a longing he'd been trying to deny.

An attraction he'd tried to ignore. To distance himself from. A woman who had invaded his thoughts from the get-go, thoughts he was unable to shake free from since.

He shifted his weight enough so that his hand was free to grab her. To feel her. His fingers wrapped around her hip. He pulled her up against him and felt her breath hitch against his lips.

Caleb wanted to deepen the kiss. He wanted to explore more of her.

But he also knew it wasn't the time.

With more self-control than he thought he had, he gently pulled away.

Alyssa was trying to catch her breath, her pink, pink lips darkened from the contact and her blue eyes focusing on him.

"You two okay back there?" called their driver, foot still pressed hard on the gas pedal.

"I'm okay," Alyssa finally answered for the both of them. Her voice was ragged but stronger than it had been.

Caleb waited a beat, still caught in her blue-eyed stare, before he answered, "I'm okay too." Finally he tore his gaze from the woman and focused on the driver in the front seat. "Thanks for the save, Sheriff."

Sheriff Reed didn't take his attention off the street, but when he answered there was no doubt in Caleb's mind that the man was smiling.

"It's what I do."

IT WAS LIKE her life was now made up of moments that were either on the extreme side of the danger spectrum or floundering in a deep calm. Though, sitting in the conference room at the sheriff's department, trying to make out the blurs on the whiteboard across from her, Alyssa thought maybe calm wasn't the right choice of words.

She let a sigh out that no one heard. It was the first time she'd been alone since the sheriff rescued them. Even though he'd brought deputies on his tail, they still hadn't been able to capture Norman. Or Dupree, for that matter. Which was the main reason it was now seven in the morning and she was still at the department. Everyone on the force seemed to be out on the streets, hunting down the two men. Dupree they knew, but his connection with Norman and who Norman was, well, that was the mystery. One that she wished she could help solve.

Another sigh climbed out of her mouth and through her lips. She traced them with the tips of her fingers.

In all the madness that had happened, how did she always come back to a kiss?

Two kisses, actually, she thought, cheeks heating while somewhere lower warmed. She couldn't forget that one she'd planted on the unsuspecting deputy. No, she definitely couldn't forget that.

Or the fact that he'd responded.

In more ways than one.

If it had been up to her, she would have let the deputy take her right then and there, sheriff in the front seat and all. She'd been so relieved and happy to see him in the house. That enthusiasm had waited until she felt even a small amount of safety.

And then she had needed to let him know how she felt about it.

"More important things," Alyssa whispered to the empty room. "Focus."

"What was that?"

Alyssa jumped and looked at the new body in the room. The image might be blurry, but Alyssa knew it was the dispatcher, Cassie. The woman had already stopped by when she first came in to work to check on her. Thanks to her, Alyssa was also wearing a pair of exercise pants and not her sleep shorts. Which somehow had made her feel better. Or, at the very least, a little more in control of the situation.

"Oh, nothing," Alyssa hurried, the heat of her blush getting a little hotter. "Just, you know, talking to myself to keep awake."

"Well, I think I might be able to help with that!"

Alyssa smelled the coffee before she even saw the cup.

"The perk of being across the street from a coffee shop," Cassie added. She leaned against the table's edge, closer than if she'd taken the seat next to Alyssa. Which was probably on purpose so she wasn't a blur in her vision.

Alyssa hoped after all this was over that she'd become friends with the dispatcher.

If Alyssa survived the madness.

"I know this is a weird thing to bring up right now," Alyssa started. "But I wanted to thank you for the advice." Cassie raised her eyebrow in question. "For telling me to request Caleb for protection. I, well, I don't know how everything would have played out otherwise."

Cassie's lips curved up into a small smile. "I'm glad he's worked out for you. He seems to be a good guy." Her expression dampened. "It'll be a shame when he goes back to Portland. The department will suffer for it."

Alyssa had spent the last few days stumbling upon realizations that had turned her blood cold. However, Cassie had just shared information that had a parallel, if not equal, effect on her. More than anything she'd bet that Eleanor had been trying to tell her the same thing she'd just learned before the explosion that had killed Ted happened.

That Caleb didn't plan on staying in Carpenter.

And why would he?

Feeling her face harden into what she hoped was a normal smile, Alyssa nodded.

Voices floating down the hallway toward the conference room saved Alyssa from having to pretend she wasn't upset. Disappointed was not a strong enough word.

"Well, speak of the devil," Cassie greeted Caleb. He was holding a duffel bag and looked as tightly wound as could be. Alyssa couldn't blame him for that. But she also couldn't meet his eye at the moment. Not when the news of him eventually leaving hurt more than she was comfortable with. Instead she deferred her attention to Captain Jones behind him.

"Anything?"

The captain shook his head. Despite his earlier grievances with Caleb, he didn't seem to have any undue anger radiating off him. Instead there was an intense focus that Alyssa was finding synonymous with the Riker County Sheriff's Department.

"Nothing concrete," he answered. "And not Norman or Dupree. We've even looked everywhere you suggested that you found Dupree frequented when looking into him last year."

"Maybe they've left Carpenter altogether," Alyssa pointed out. Though she didn't want to see either man again, she realized the danger of them possibly never being caught would increase if they left town.

It was Caleb's turn to shake his head.

"There's a reason Dupree didn't leave when he had the chance," he said. "Whatever plan Norman was talking to you about must be keeping them here until it's finished."

"Not to mention Norman—" the captain started, but he cut himself off right after.

Alyssa let out her third sigh in a handful of minutes.

"Norman seems to want me," she finished for him.

"Which might be a good thing," Captain Jones said. "It could keep them in town, which gives us the time to complete our search and find them. It's not ideal, but none of this is."

"Captain." A female deputy stopped in the doorway. "Sorry to interrupt, but Chief Hawser would like a word with you. He's on hold in your office."

"Okay, thank you." Jones turned to Caleb. "If you need anything, don't hesitate to let me know. The sheriff too."

Caleb nodded. A look passed between the men, but without her glasses Alyssa couldn't tell if it was a good one or not.

"I also need to get back to it," Cassie said at her elbow. "I just wanted to make sure you had some caffeine in you."

Alyssa smiled.

"And I thank you for that," she said. "And the pants."

Cassie patted her shoulder and followed the captain out. Then it was just the two of them.

Alyssa couldn't avoid the deputy anymore. "So, what now?"

Chapter Eighteen

If you had told Alyssa the week before that she'd be naked in Deputy Caleb Foster's house, she would have laughed. Not to mention ask who Caleb Foster was. Staring at her reflection in his bathroom mirror, she marveled at the fact that she'd never even known he had existed until a few days ago. Now there she was, freshly showered and contemplating her relationship with the man a few rooms over.

That was one of many curveballs she hadn't been prepared for in the slightest. The others being the still unknown man who was Norman, her nightmare incarnate Dupree and their joint, mystery plan that either did or did not involve her. All during a week that should have been spent putting away the Storm Chasers once and for all.

Alyssa hoped she'd eventually be able to hit all those life curveballs.

In the distance the *clink* of dishes broke her out of her reverie. She grabbed the towel and dried the rest of the way off before diving into the duffel bag Caleb had packed while she was at the department. At the time she hadn't known the deputy was going to her house but was grateful he had. Along with clothes, toiletries and a pair of shoes, he'd managed to find her spare set of glasses, beneath the couch of all places.

Slipping them on had reduced her anxiety by half. It was one thing to be scared. It was another to be blind *and* scared.

Alyssa changed into a pair of sports shorts and a plain T-shirt. She might have gotten a few hours of sleep the night before, but it hadn't been enough to replenish any exhaustion caused by the chaos that had come after. Unless it was absolutely necessary, she planned on staying put for the time being. Caleb had assured her that the captain and sheriff had assured *him* that they would be the first to know if any break in the case happened. On the off chance Dupree and Norman tried to track Alyssa down again, there was an undercover black-and-white car outside on high alert. So, until that break came, all they had to do was wait.

Which made her anxious for another reason.

Alyssa sucked on her lip and exited the bathroom.

"Thanks again for letting me stay here," she greeted the deputy when she got enough courage to walk into the living room. He was settled on the couch, so she took the chair at his side. Close but not too close.

"I'm just returning the favor," he said with a shrug. "You opened your home to me more than once already."

Alyssa's face began to heat at the thought of his hand gripping her body, feeling the beginnings of his arousal pressing against the thin material of her sleep shorts.

But then just as quickly she remembered Cassie's words.

He was leaving Carpenter.

He was leaving her.

"So, what did Deputy Mills have to say?" she asked, trying to curb her hurt before he could see he'd caused it. He'd taken a call from the man just before she excused herself to go shower.

"It was actually from his father, but he said Dante will be fine." He pointed to his cheek. "He has a hairline fracture but nothing permanent. When he was awake he told the captain that Dupree used the butt of his gun to knock him out. He didn't even hear the man coming."

"It's a good thing he did that instead of shoot," she pointed out. The spot on her back that was puckered from her scar tingled. "He hasn't always been reserved about doing that."

Caleb nodded. She noticed his jaw hardened.

"I can only assume he decided against it so he could try to sneak around me. It was bad and good timing he got to your house when he did. Otherwise he might have taken you before we even realized he had escaped the transport."

"That should be a silver lining to look at, but when it comes to Dupree, I'm not too thrilled about it," she admitted. "But I am glad you were there. I'd much rather have been grabbed by Norman than Dupree. As weird as *that* sounds."

Alyssa tried on her best "I'm all right" smile, but Caleb already looked like he wasn't buying it. She let a sigh drag her body down. "The way Norman talked to me… I don't think he would have hurt me. I mean, he could have done whatever he wanted with me, but he didn't."

Caleb puffed up as if he had an air pump attached to him. "Just because he didn't do anything to you doesn't mean he's a good guy. You *were* kidnapped."

Alyssa couldn't help giving a small eye roll. "I know, I know." She dropped her gaze to the coffee table. Sports magazines were stacked on top of it, being one of the few bits of proof someone inhabited the rental house. It only reminded Alyssa that Caleb's stay wasn't permanent. Which made her feel somehow awkward when she continued, "It's just that, well, Norman seems to be in love with me. Or, at least, *thinks* he is. Which is another thing I don't understand at all."

From her periphery she watched Caleb loosen a little.

"I don't think it's that hard to grasp that a man fell for you," he said, voice serious.

Her cheeks heated for the umpteenth time. She started to open her mouth to stop him.

"You're brave and smart," he continued, cutting her off. "You took a bullet trying to save a man you hardly knew. You ran into a burning building to try to save someone who *might* have still been alive. You blindly fought your captor to escape without any help from me. You did all that and still took the time to show concern about Robbie and Eleanor and the rest of the witnesses before showing concern about yourself." Caleb moved to the edge of the couch, teetering on standing or, in her mind, reaching out to her. But he kept the distance as he finished. "I might not know you like the rest of this town does, but I *do* understand how easy it would be to fall for you."

Alyssa's lips froze. What she had been about to say stalled. The heat of her blush wasn't raging. Instead it moved across her body as a slow burn. It reminded her not of embarrassment but of something else. Something she'd felt when Caleb kissed her. Something she'd felt when she kissed him back in the sheriff's Bronco.

It was longing. Plain and simple.

There was no denying its place anymore. To pretend she didn't want the man in front of her was too much of a pain. He was right. She'd been through her own version of hell and back in the last year and week. Admitting she had kissed Caleb in the Bronco because she'd been so terrified she had lost him that when he was there, staring down at her, she'd realized how happy the sight had made her... Well, that didn't seem so scary now.

Still, she managed to hold back enough to correct him. With a small smile, she tucked her head a little but not her gaze. It stayed right with his mesmerizing green eyes. "I meant I don't understand why he's in love with me, considering I've never met him before."

Caleb's eyes widened a fraction. For one tense moment Alyssa thought she'd offended him by pointing out he'd given her a world of compliments because of a misunderstanding. But then a slow grin pulled up the corners of his lips.

"Ah," he said with a little laugh. "Well, I've already said what I think and I'm not going to take that back."

It was Alyssa's turn to laugh.

"I wasn't going to ask you to," she said. "It was a really nice compliment."

Caleb's grin faltered. "It's the truth."

The distance between them felt unbearably vast. Somehow the foot or two seemed almost cruel.

"You know, the past few days have put us in intense situations, and sometimes those can lead to emotions running high," Alyssa said, voice going softer the more she spoke. Was it her imagination or was the deputy leaning closer? And was she responding in the same way? "It can confuse the way people think and feel. Especially when the rush is over and everything gets back to being quiet."

Caleb leaned forward, like Alyssa was attached to him by an invisible string, and she mimicked him. The impossibly large space between them shrank until it was nonexistent. Slowly, or maybe cautiously, Caleb reached out and tucked a strand of her wet hair behind her ear. When he was done he let his knuckles brush along her jaw. His skin was warm and perfect.

"But it's in the quiet times like right now that I find you the most fascinating." Caleb grabbed her by the chin, holding her steady. Holding all of her.

And in the next second, his lips brushed against hers.

Electricity. She could have sworn she felt it between them.

Alyssa was ready for its current to carry them further, but once again, Caleb pulled away. Their kiss broke. With hooded eyes she watched as his lips parted to talk.

"I—I'm sorry," he said, pulling farther back. "I shouldn't have—"

Alyssa watched as the certainty of his actions fell away. It created such strong disappointment within her that Alyssa jumped up off the chair.

"It's fine," she interrupted, the heat in her cheeks now complete embarrassment. It prompted her to blurt out the first thing that popped into her head. "We can count it as a goodbye kiss."

Whatever Caleb was about to say caught in his throat. He raised an eyebrow but couldn't hide a look she knew well.

Guilt.

"Cassie told me that you're going back to Portland," she explained. The look of guilt worsened.

"Eventually," he finally said. "That's the plan."

Never had she disliked four words more.

She took a deep breath and mustered up a smile.

"Then I guess it's good we went ahead and got that out of the way," she said, already angling her body to head to the guest bedroom. It was set up as an office, but there was a couch inside. That was all she needed to lick her wounds in private. "You know, I'm pretty beat anyways. I think I'm going to lie down for a little bit, if that's okay."

She was already walking away, but Caleb still answered. "Maybe it's a good idea if we both get a little sleep."

Alyssa nodded, felt stupid for nodding and fled to

the bedroom. There she shut the door and put her back against it.

It's for the best, she thought.

She pushed herself off the door but didn't make it two steps before it opened again. Alyssa turned, confused.

Caleb's eyes were wide, his chest heaving. He looked every bit like a man trying to restrain himself. From what, though, was something Alyssa wanted—*needed*—to know. She felt her eyebrow rise.

"The other day you said that not everyone stays," he started. "Yeah, that might be true. People leave for all kinds of reasons. And I might not have known you that long, but—" he took a step forward "—no matter what happens, I want you to know that you are one of the only reasons that I'd ever stay."

Caleb's hands found their way across the space between them and into her hair. They pulled her face to him again. Just like he had done after escaping the house. Just like she had done to him after getting away from Norman.

His tongue parted her lips and this time around neither pulled away after a few seconds.

Caleb moved his hands down her sides and then pulled her against him in an embrace that put her flush against him. Alyssa wrapped her arms around him as the kiss deepened. Her body began to thrum at every movement. It was a feeling that she wanted to add fire to, so when he used his embrace to lift her off the floor, she wrapped her legs around his waist.

Alyssa had thought there was nothing more the man

could say or do to make her want him more. But, somehow, Caleb Foster did it.

He walked them to his bedroom, put her on the bed and broke their kiss. Through hooded lashes Alyssa watched as the man smiled a smile that sealed her fate.

"Oh boy," she whispered.

Caleb's smile widened. He kicked off his shoes and threw his shirt to the floor. Alyssa didn't even pretend she wasn't checking the man out. His finely toned chest dipped into abs that didn't seem real before a light dusting of golden hair headed south to the hem of his jeans.

"Well, *hello*, Deputy Foster," she breathed.

Caleb's smile turned mischievous. She answered his with an offer of her own. Without hesitation Alyssa pulled her shirt over her head and threw it. Caleb also wasn't for pretending he wasn't tracing her body with his eyes. Belatedly she realized that the red-and-black-lace bra she had on was one that he himself had packed for her earlier that morning.

"Well, hello, Miss Garner."

Alyssa's heart was thumping against her chest as Caleb took charge. He moved onto the bed with purpose until he was hovering over her. Then his mouth was on her lips. Then on her shoulder. Then her collarbone.

His lips left a trail of raised flesh as they moved across her skin. She arced upward, moaning as they reached her cleavage. He used the arc to his advantage and slipped his hand behind her back. She was too aroused to care at how easily he unclipped her bra. All she knew was that she was grateful when it loosened. It gave Caleb enough room to move one cup aside. He chafed his thumb over her nipple in a tantalizing rhythm.

Alyssa couldn't take it any longer. She pulled his lips back up to hers and moaned. Of its own accord her body began to pulse against his, wanting—needing—more. If the hardness pressing against her was any indication, she wasn't the only one who was hungry.

She had moved her hands from around his neck, down the sides of his arms, more than ready to rid the man of his pants, when her fingers ran over something she didn't expect. Confused, she pulled away.

He hovered above her, eyebrow raised.

"What happened here?" she whispered, eyes tracing over his bare biceps. Two butterfly bandages were over a deep cut. It was covered in dried blood.

Caleb managed to shrug.

"Caleb?" she prodded.

He sighed.

"A bullet grazed me earlier," he admitted. "When we were running from the house."

Alyssa felt her eyes widen.

"It's just a graze and I'm okay. The most it will do is scar."

Alyssa felt a heaviness in her chest.

"You were shot because of me," she said, her mood darkening despite a body strung out with pure arousal. "You could have been really hurt, or worse."

Caleb's expression softened. He lowered his lips and brushed them gently across hers. He pulled back to meet her gaze again.

"But I wasn't," he whispered. He lowered himself again, but this time his lips trailed down to her hardened nipple. She tried to restrain a moan as he kissed the tip. When he looked up at her and spoke, his breath against her skin sent a chill across her body. It made her ache in all the best ways. "And right now, Miss Garner, I'm here. With you."

The space between them dissolved, replaced by a desire neither could ignore. Caleb resumed kissing every part of her before each had found a way to undress the other. Alyssa opened herself to the man, and Caleb pressed against her until both were caught in a whirlwind of heat and friction and pleasure.

Lust, longing and something undefinable created a dance between them that kept all thoughts and emotions occupied.

Norman, Dupree Slater and Carpenter became distant memories.

All that was left was this one room.

Chapter Nineteen

Warm.

Quiet.

Blurry.

Alyssa's world might have been filled with fear and danger and so much uncertainty it should have had her locked in constant panic, but the moment she woke up in Caleb's bed, all she could feel was contentment.

She rolled over, trying to be as quiet as possible. Even without her glasses she was surprised to be able to make out Caleb's face in detail.

A smile split her lips. It was because he was so close to her. Within the small bubble that was her field of good vision. Alyssa couldn't remember the last time someone had been that close to her, especially in bed.

That thought prompted a rush of heat to move up from below her waistline. It settled in her neck and cheeks. She'd known the man entangled with her beneath his sheets for a handful of days and yet…

She searched his slack face, knowing she shouldn't feel what she did. While awake his expression so often switched between a quiet burden and a loud concern, but the sleeping man she was looking at now had found peace. It might not extend past his eyes being opened, but for the moment, he seemed to have found it.

Alyssa chanced stroking his cheek. Lying on his stomach, arm tossed over her middle and legs tangled with hers, he didn't move an inch as she did so. She absently wondered when the last time he'd gotten good sleep was.

A loud series of beeping snuffed out her current thoughts. Caleb's body went from relaxed and comfortable to coiled and tense all within one moment. Two green eyes, perfectly rimmed with gold, found hers.

"I think it's your phone," she said, nodding to the other side of the bed.

Where she'd thrown his pants.

Right next to where he'd thrown her shorts.

She had no idea where her undergarments had wound up.

Alyssa's cheeks heated again as Caleb pulled his arm off her bare skin and moved his attention to the other side of the bed. His phone belted out another series of high-pitched beeps. He muttered under his breath and pitched over the side to swat for his phone. In the process the sheets shifted and Alyssa was presented with an unobstructed view of the man's very bare backside. It was slightly blurry but still just as perfect as it had been a few hours before.

"Foster," he grunted, pulling his upper body back onto the bed. It shifted the sheets again and exposed Alyssa's naked chest. There was a soreness around her nipples, but she in no way disliked it. Still, she hurried to cover herself, suddenly uncertain. They'd both melted into the heat of passion. Skin on skin, heat with heat, lust and hunger and a singular attention only for each other... But now their fire had had time to cool. What if it never happened again? What if this was the first and last time she ever felt him?

Alyssa tamped down her worries while the man on the other end of the phone rattled off information with alarming speed.

"Got it," Caleb finally said, voice tight. "No, no problem. Thank you."

He ended the call.

"Did they find Norman or Dupree?" Alyssa asked, hopeful.

Caleb turned to face her, keeping on his stomach. She fought the urge to blush again.

"No," he said. "But the sheriff promised me he'd let me know when Robbie and Eleanor made it to their son's house. And they did and are fine."

Alyssa let out a sigh of relief. While Robbie had been quick to refuse leaving town, Dupree's escape had put pressure on his decision to stay. Especially since Dupree had chased Robbie most of the way to the police station, shooting up his truck as they went. Together Alyssa and Caleb had been able to persuade both Rickmans that maybe out of town *was* the safest option for them. And, to both their surprise, Cassie had been given orders to drive them to their son's when they'd agreed. However, before they'd left, Eleanor tried her best to sway Alyssa into going with them, but everyone knew that was a pointless fight.

Whoever Norman was he clearly wanted Alyssa. Their best bet of capturing him was to stay in Carpenter. If she left, Alyssa had no doubt that Norman would follow. At least in Carpenter they were on her home turf. It was easier to look over your shoulder while navigating the familiar. Plus, there was no denying she felt safer with the naked deputy next to her.

"I didn't mean to sleep this long," Caleb said, jumping topics. His gaze went back to his phone, but she caught his grin. "I didn't mean to sleep at all, to be honest."

"My guess is that you needed to recharge."

Just as quickly as Alyssa said it, she felt her cheeks flame. She wanted to stick her head in the sand like the awkward woman she was. "Because, you know, you haven't slept in a while. That's why you needed the recharge."

Caleb's grin widened.

"I definitely got a charge of something," he said with a wink.

More heat thrummed through her from below her stomach. The sheets covering them seemed impossibly thin and yet cumbersome. She resisted the urge to throw them off, waiting to see what the deputy would do next.

She wasn't disappointed.

Pushing himself up on his forearms, he met her stare easily enough. So close she could feel his breath against her. The same breath that had trailed across her body. His lips, soft when needed and hard when wanted, pulled up out of a grin and into a smirk. It exuded nothing but an exciting mischievousness. She saw it in wonderful detail. It prompted another unfiltered response from her. "I like when you're this close so you're not a blur."

Caleb moved in until his lips were over hers.

Soft. Warm. Brimming with promise she didn't know she'd wanted. Her body started to arc up, responding to the hope that the kiss would extend past just one kiss when a foreign noise cut through the air.

Caleb laughed against her as another growl sounded.

"Sorry," he said. "I guess sleep wasn't the only thing I was lacking." He pulled away and rolled over, tapping his stomach. "I think the last good meal I had was Eleanor's leftover pie."

Slightly disappointed, Alyssa realized she hadn't eaten in a while either. But watching Caleb untangle himself from the sheets, she pondered the importance of eating versus the desire to keep the deputy naked.

"How about I go make us some food?" he asked, picking up his jeans and shimmying back into them. His shirt remained off. She wasn't about to complain.

"You won't hear me arguing," she said. "Especially if by food you also mean coffee?"

The cup she'd gotten from Cassie in the early morning hours hadn't dented her exhaustion. Even the sleep she'd just woken from hadn't relieved her of the desire to lie back down.

Caleb laughed again.

"Not only do I have coffee," he said, his smile slightly blurred. "But I have some of the best you'll ever taste. Thanks to my old chief, it's straight from Portland."

Alyssa felt her stomach drop.

She tried to keep her expression from going down with it.

"Great," she exclaimed, attempting to recover and be convincing. "Sounds great!" Trying to pretend that the mention of Portland alone hadn't thrust her back into a reality she didn't want to be a part of at all. One where Caleb was only a temporary resident in Carpenter. "I'm going to go freshen up and then take Sergeant out to stretch," she added when Caleb seemed to have stalled beside the bed.

If he was going to say something, Alyssa didn't give him the chance. Without asking, she wrapped the sheet around herself, grabbed her bag and hurried into the bathroom. Once the door was closed she immediately went to turn on the shower. It muffled any sounds that were outside the room.

Alyssa waited to see if the deputy would come for her like he had before. To try to comfort the part of her that was hurt by the idea that he would leave her, eventually. But he never did. So she did as she said and freshened up, changed into jeans and a shirt, and tried to see the poetry of having at least known what being with the deputy was like. Even if it might never happen again.

It took a little time, but she felt she was starting to convince herself that it was fine in her book when she got up to the mirror to brush out her hair. She took a towel and tried to un-fog a circle of space so she could see her reflection. It was an action she was used to handling when it came to her glasses and the often humid weather of Alabama. Something so natural to her that she often did it on autopilot whether she was at home or out and about.

Alyssa froze midwipe.

An idea grew louder in her head. It was attached to a memory. One she hadn't thought was important.

Until now.

CALEB LOOKED AT the plate across the counter from his own. It was small and chipped and a part of a set he'd had for years… Yet somehow that plate looked different now.

Holding eggs, bacon and toast, it was a sight that he hadn't expected to make him contemplate his life. But that was what he was doing. Because he knew it wasn't the plate that had changed all of a sudden. It was who the plate was meant for that had cracked his plan for an ideal future.

He saw the plate.

He saw the woman meant to eat off it.

Caleb exhaled above his coffee.

Yet another small detail that had changed the way he thought.

He replayed Alyssa's reaction to when he'd mentioned Portland. Even in the smallest way. The way her face had fallen for a second as she, no doubt, was reminded that he was going to leave. He didn't know what bothered him more after seeing that. Hurting her with the truth of going back or the idea of going back itself.

A series of memories reminded him of a night he never wished to relive again. A darkness he hoped to keep buried for life. His hands fisted.

He knew it wasn't that easy.

If he stayed he'd have to tell Alyssa what had happened. He'd have to show her he wasn't the man she thought she knew. But if he left?

She'd never know.

Blue eyes, soft skin, hair that smelled like citrus.

Caleb opened his hands back up.

If he left, he'd be leaving behind every part of the woman he'd gotten to know in the last week. The strength and humor and compassion. The quiet contemplation, the way her brow creased in worry and the blushes that colored her cheeks that he seemed to have a skill to incite.

The way her skin felt against his. Their bodies moving together and against each other at the same time. The soft moans. The eventual release.

He might have been uncertain about a lot of things in life, but Caleb knew, without a doubt, that if he left he'd never find another woman like Alyssa Garner again.

And he wouldn't want to.

Footsteps made him turn around. Alyssa was dressed again and also wearing a look that worried him.

"What's wrong?"

Alyssa's eyebrows were drawn together, her forehead creased in thought, but her expression was hard. And oddly energetic.

"Stand here," she hurried, grabbing his hand and pulling him to the middle of the room. "I want to try something."

Caleb obeyed and watched as she took her glasses off. Without explanation, Alyssa moved a few steps backward and then walked forward again. She bumped into his shoulder but kept on walking past him. Curious, he turned his head to look at her. She stopped a foot away from him, brows drawn even tighter together.

She squinted.

"Alyssa?" he prodded. "What's wrong?"

For a moment she didn't speak.

And then she said something that changed everything. "I think I *have* met Norman before. He was there, Caleb."

He turned to face her head-on.

"There?" he asked, already hoping for information that could help them close the case once and for all.

Alyssa gave one, decisive nod. As if she was confirming her hunch with herself before letting him in on it.

"He was at the bank," she said. "The day of the robbery, Norman was there."

Chapter Twenty

"Just tell them what you told me."

Caleb's hand touched the top of hers with reassurance. No one else in the conference room at the sheriff's department could see the contact beneath the table. But it helped steady her all the same.

Alyssa straightened her back and cleared her throat. "Before the robbery took place, when I was first going into the bank, my glasses fogged up." As if the sheriff and captain needed help understanding the information, she motioned to her glasses. "It was raining and so humid I knew it was pointless to try to wipe them off until I was inside. So I took them off and held them at my side so no one would see me looking clumsily around while I waited for the fog to disappear. I was so focused on trying to look like I wasn't blind that before I put them back on I ran into a man in the lobby. He was leaving, but we hit each other hard enough that we both turned to look at one another." This time she took her glasses off and returned her gaze to the two men on the other side of the table. "You two are blurs right now. Even if you pointed a gun to my head, without having seen you before *with* my glasses on, I couldn't for the life of me describe what you look like. Other than with descriptions like tall, brown hair and wearing a suit, I wouldn't be able to recognize you later either."

Alyssa put her glasses back on just in time to watch Sheriff Reed catch on.

"And you think it was Norman that you ran into," he guessed. "In the bank."

Alyssa nodded.

"It would explain why Dupree came into the room she was being held in and broke her glasses," Caleb interjected. "He was trying to prove to Norman that even though she might have looked at him, she didn't really see him. Which is in line with the conversation between him and Norman she heard."

The captain was already standing.

"I have a copy of the security footage from the bank in my office," he said to the sheriff. "I'll go see if I can find this man."

Sheriff Reed nodded but didn't split his attention. He kept it right on Alyssa.

"If it is the same man, that still doesn't fill in all the blanks," he said. "So let's say Norman did bump into you at the bank and it was the first time you two met... What he said to you when you were at that house sounds like he's in love with you. *And* he seems to be under the impression that you are in love with him too. Or at least in the same reality together. Now, I'm not one to discount the notion of love at first sight, believe you me—I was knocked on my backside when I first saw my wife—but what Norman seems to be feeling might be something a great deal more dangerous."

"Obsession," Caleb jumped in.

The sheriff nodded, grave.

"Obsession, especially within the walls of an unstable mind, can be even more dangerous than someone who is just mad at the world or, as Norman told you, out for revenge," Sheriff Reed said. He put his hands together in a show of binding two objects. "But put those two together?"

He whistled and shook his head.

Alyssa cleared her throat. While she'd given the two men in the room with her a breakdown of everything both Dupree and Norman had said to and in front of her, she had sidestepped one particular statement. In hindsight she realized it was to try to keep the then-angry Caleb from getting even more angry. Now, though, it felt pertinent.

"Norman said Dupree helped prove we were meant to be together," she began, already feeling uncomfortable. "I don't think he became obsessed with me until he realized I survived."

Caleb squeezed her hand. Whether it was meant to calm her or protect her she didn't know.

"Okay, so let's say you bump into Norman, make eye contact—which starts this crazy notion you two should be together—and then you get…well, you know."

"Hospitalized," Caleb offered. In a different situation Alyssa might have thought it was cute how both men were trying to sidestep the gritty facts of that day for her benefit.

"Yeah, so you get hospitalized and Norman realizes that you've survived," the sheriff continued. "In his mind that means you two are meant for each other, creating an obsession that he adds into his plans for, as he said it, his revenge."

"That would explain why Dupree seemed so mad," she added. "Maybe it's affecting their partnership."

"Which in itself is another set of questions we don't have answers for," Caleb pointed out. "If Norman was at the bank, then why didn't he help rob it? For that matter, why did he go in at all beforehand and without a mask?"

"And why is he blowing people up?" Alyssa tacked on.

"And what revenge is he talking about?" the sheriff asked. "His partners being killed and caught?"

"That's a lot of questions, but I think I can at least answer one for you."

In unison the three of them turned to Captain Jones in the doorway.

"I found the man who bumped into you on the tape. It's Norman," he confirmed. "From your descriptions of him now, he appears to be more cleanly cut from the footage, but it's him. Glasses and everything."

Alyssa didn't know if that should have made her happy, but in a small way it did. Better to know what was going on than be in the dark any longer.

"But—" the captain started. What small amount of happiness had cropped up within Alyssa disappeared.

Apparently she wasn't the only one. Caleb let go of her hand.

"We may have another problem," Jones finished.

Without saying a word, they followed the man back to his office and crowded around him as he sat in front of his computer. Alyssa sucked in a breath.

It wasn't that she saw herself on the monitor, frozen in time right in front of an also-paused Norman, that caught her off guard.

"We had no idea what was about to happen," she whispered. An old pain ached within her. This time Caleb didn't hide his attempt to make her feel better. He put his hand on the small of her back. The pressure was comforting. She took a deep breath.

"But that's him, right?" the captain asked to make sure.

It was Caleb who nodded. "That's him."

"And that must be the look he was talking about," the sheriff jumped in. He pointed to the screen. Alyssa tried to focus on it and not the dam that kept her memories at bay starting to crack.

"You can see my glasses in my hand," she said after a tiny head shake to help get her back into a more stable mind-set. Past Alyssa was a good two feet away from Past Norman. "If I'd only left them on instead of worrying about how I looked, I would never have bumped into him in the first place. And y'all wouldn't be in harm's way because of me."

"Don't blame yourself for the crazy in others," Sheriff Reed said. "Plus, I don't think his obsession for you is what made him start making bombs and using them. It also doesn't explain what his connection with Dupree is."

Captain Jones held up his index finger. "I have a theory."

The captain hit a few keys on the keyboard until the security footage rewound. Alyssa watched her past self, as well as Norman, leave the bank in reverse until he hit Play.

"You see this is when Norman enters," he said, letting his finger trail the man on the screen. "He doesn't hesitate or break his stride as he goes to talk to one of the tellers. He has a plan."

"That's Larissa," Alyssa realized. A lump started to form in her throat as she watched Norman and Larissa talk. The teller was smiling wide, polite. Alyssa tried to ignore the sorrow while pointing out the teller to Caleb. "She didn't survive the robbery."

No one said anything for a moment. Alyssa took the time to say a silent prayer for the woman and those she left behind.

"Okay, so what's the theory?" Sheriff Reed finally asked.

There was no denying that a new thread of anger had woven itself into the fabric of the room. Caleb's hand was still on the small of her back, but the gentle nature had taken on more of an edge. The other two had shoulders lined with tension.

Captain Jones rewound the tape and pointed to Norman. Or, rather, the briefcase in his hand.

"You see this?" Jones asked. "He walks in with it."

He fast-forwarded the footage and hit Pause again. It was right before Alyssa had bumped into him. "But now…"

Alyssa watched as Past Norman left Larissa's line and headed to the hallway that led to the bathroom. The captain moved the footage along until Norman reappeared in the lobby.

Without his briefcase.

"So he left the case in the bathroom," Caleb said. "And I'm guessing he doesn't go back for it?"

Captain Jones shook his head. He'd let the security footage continue to play. Alyssa watched as another bank-goer caught Norman's eye and started a conversation with the man. It wasn't a long conversation but seemed pleasant if their easy smiles were any indication of the mood.

Currently, Alyssa's own mood was nose-diving.

"That's Carl," she said, cutting off whatever Captain Jones was about to say. "He's talking to Carl Redford." Alyssa's gut turned cold.

"Carl also didn't make it," Sheriff Reed explained to, she assumed, Caleb. The deputy opened his mouth to say something, but Alyssa cut him off.

"Does he talk to anyone else before leaving?" she asked, heartbeat speeding up.

The captain fast-forwarded the footage again in answer. He stopped it when Alyssa showed up on the screen. "Just you."

Caleb's hand dropped from her back. They shared a look.

"The only three people Norman talked to were shot

by Dupree during the robbery," he said, voice steel. "That can't be a coincidence."

"I *knew* it wasn't an accident that he shot Larissa and Carl," Alyssa agreed.

"He could have been acting under orders from Norman to take out anyone who might be able to remember him inside the bank," Caleb added.

Sheriff Reed cursed beneath his breath.

"But why go through all that trouble when we can just look at the security footage?" Alyssa asked. "Why walk into the bank without a mask on at all?" None of what they were finding was making complete sense. They were only getting pieces that weren't quite fitting together.

"It was such a cut-and-dry case that we didn't pore over the security footage with the same attention to detail we would have if the robbers hadn't been caught," the sheriff admitted. "Dupree claimed leadership for the crew and took responsibility for creating the plan to rob the bank and executing it. We had no reason to suspect there was another party to contend with." He motioned to the monitor with an angry enthusiasm. "Norman might as well have been invisible."

"But his briefcase isn't," Caleb interjected. "Maybe if we can find out where it went, we can—"

"We can figure out why he was there in the first place," Sheriff Reed continued.

Caleb nodded.

"Am I the only one who thinks the bank robbery might not have been a normal bank robbery?" Alyssa couldn't help asking. Norman just didn't *fit* into the situation. It didn't make sense.

"Whatever is going on, we'll get to the bottom of it," the sheriff assured her. He patted Jones's shoulder once. "Can you keep going through the footage? Now that we have a new perspective, maybe there's more we missed originally."

"Sure thing." Captain Jones rewound the footage again. This time Alyssa didn't want to watch. It all made her stomach turn.

"As much as I want to dig into this, I need to focus on the present," Sheriff Reed continued, walking them out. "I'm going to go back to heading up the search for Dupree and Norman. I'll be damned if I'm going to let the two of them run wild in my town."

Chapter Twenty-One

Alyssa stopped the sheriff before he headed out to try to save the day. Caleb kept to her side. She doubted she'd be able to shake him again until Dupree and Norman were caught. Not that she was particularly excited to do that.

"I thought you were working a case out of town?"

She remembered what Cassie had told her in the hospital and couldn't help asking the man about it. She felt obligated to check in with him, considering he'd saved her and Caleb's backsides earlier. "Did you finish it up already?"

A shadow of emotion crossed the sheriff's face. It made her wish she hadn't asked at all. He shook his head.

"My chief deputy and lead detective are still working it," he said. "It's an old case, but we're hoping to wrap it up sooner rather than later."

Caleb perked up at that. "I thought you were done with it and that's why you came back to town."

Sheriff Reed smiled. It was a sad look. "No matter where I am or what I'm doing, you just don't get away with attacking my home. It's as simple as that. After I heard what had happened, nothing could have kept me from coming back. Plus, I had a hunch you wouldn't listen to Jones's telling you to go home and rest. I figured backup was just the thing you might need. As long as you're a part of my team, that's the very least I can offer you."

Alyssa felt a genuine smile spring to her lips. An infusion of pride blossomed inside her chest at the conviction behind his words.

"Now, I need you two to keep a low profile until we get a break in this case."

Caleb opened his mouth to, she assumed, protest, but the sheriff cut him off. "Before you say anything, I want you to know I'm not benching you because of protocol. I'm just asking you to keep her out of the sights of two unstable men while we work the case. Okay? That's not the same thing. She's a part of this wild web, an important part that we can't afford to let go."

Caleb shut his mouth. He gave a curt nod.

"Let me know if you need anything," the sheriff said, turning to her. "And I'm sorry this is all happening. I know from experience it's not fun to be this close to a case like this. We'll catch them and make sure they pay for everything they've done. Sheriff's honor."

"Thank you," Alyssa said, sincere.

The sheriff gave a parting nod and walked deeper into the department. The badge on his belt shone as the light caught it when he turned. Alyssa followed Caleb out into the lobby, still smiling.

"You know, I voted for him," she whispered at his

shoulder, the feeling of pride for the sheriff carrying into her words. "He's a good man."

Caleb made a show of looking back to the hallway. He shrugged.

"I guess he's okay. You know, if you're into that tall, dark and rugged thing," Caleb deadpanned. It made Alyssa laugh.

"Is that jealousy I hear?" she teased, walking out the door he was holding open. She caught his grin.

"What do I have to be jealous about? I mean, have you seen these guns?" He made an exaggerated show of flexing his arms. Alyssa had to admit she liked seeing a more playful side of him. It was a nice break from the somberness that came from being in constant danger.

"Of course I've seen them. I'm betting on those things to keep me safe," she joked. It made the deputy's grin widen. Another welcome sight.

"You're about to see them drive us right back on to my place, where they'll then shovel some kind of food into my mouth." He grasped his stomach in exaggerated pain. She laughed.

"You were the one who threw out our breakfast when I had the Norman epiphany," she pointed out.

He shrugged.

"I got excited," he defended. His smile dropped. "Well, you know what I mean. Not *excited*."

"I knew what you meant," she assured him. Still, she felt slightly guilty for his hungry gut. Before she walked around to the passenger side of the car, she paused at his side. "How about *I* make us something when we get back? I don't want to brag, but while I'm sure your eggs and bacon were great, I can make a mean breakfast casserole. As long as you have some biscuits, that is."

His grin broke out into a full-on smile. It made an already attractive man that much more delicious. On reflex she began to lean in closer to him. She smelled his cologne. Had he always worn it? Or was it something new? Either way she had to actively try to keep her eyelids from closing as she savored the crisp scent.

"I guess it's lucky for me that I do."

Alyssa knew they were talking about breakfast and food, but suddenly the air between them felt charged. She imagined the body of the man in front of her sans clothes. The way he had touched her, held her. The memory alone started to heat her up.

Maybe she wasn't the only one.

Caleb's eyes moved to her lips.

And they looked just as hungry.

Just like that, a switch seemed to flip beneath Caleb's exterior. She didn't have time to be concerned about it before he bent down and pressed his lips against hers. The kiss didn't last long, but it was enough to make her desire for him burn bright. "But first, I need to tell you something. Something about my past I should have told you already."

Guilt.

Alyssa read that emotion as if a sky writer had flown it across the sky.

It sounded an alarm bell in her mind so loudly that she took a small step back.

Which gave her the perfect vantage point to see Norman walking up behind the deputy.

And he was smiling.

It only took a second for Caleb to know Norman was behind him. Alyssa's face became a mirror, showing him a look of surprise that wasn't at all a happy one. Fear was there too, but not nearly as much as if Dupree had been the culprit. Caleb reached for his gun and whirled around, careful to keep Alyssa behind him.

The bastard was showing teeth.

"Shoot and they die," he greeted the end of Caleb's gun. The man didn't even flinch at its presence. Alyssa did, judging by the small intake of breath Caleb heard. He guessed it was more for the vague threat than the tool that could end Norman's attempts to take her.

"Who dies?" she asked.

Norman tilted his head to the side to see Alyssa better. Caleb's finger itched. Only a few feet separated him and Norman. How easy it would be to end the man wasn't lost on him.

"Do you know that bombers usually only stick to one method when it comes to setting off their handiwork? Using pressure-plated bombs, for instance, has an entirely different pathology behind it than using a bomb with, say, a detonator." Norman shook his right hand at his side. There was an old flip phone open in it. "*Usually* a bomber will stick with only one method versus switching between the two." He shook his hand again. "*But* since I'm new to this I decided to try my hand at both."

He let that sink in a moment.

Caleb used that lapse to hope that whoever manned their security cameras for the department would see what was happening. They were in the side parking lot, away from the sight line to the main street and on the opposite side from the courthouse next door.

"Who dies?" Alyssa repeated. Her voice was cold but steady. Caleb wished he knew what she was thinking.

"The witnesses, of course."

Caleb's blood went cold. Surely the man was bluffing. Still, Caleb had to test him.

"You're lying," he said, gun arm not wavering. "They're all safe."

Norman bit out a chuckle.

"Why?" he asked, amused. "Because the fine Riker County law enforcement officers got them to do exactly like I wanted to do by leaving town?" Norman's laugh wasn't clipped this time. "It's easy to finish the puzzle when you can finally get to all the pieces." He shook the phone again. "But if you don't believe me I guess I could prove myself and my intentions. Who should go first, Alyssa? Missy Grayson in South Carolina with her husband? Or should I use the Rickmans' cabin in Tennessee as an example? I believe it's technically owned by their son Robert, but really, he's a Rickman too, so I suppose it's all the same."

"Why are you doing this?" Alyssa yelled. "Why continue to hurt all of us if your partner is already out of custody? *What's the point?*"

Norman was nonplussed by the emotion leaking into Alyssa's words.

"Because you care about them, Alyssa," he said simply. "And that's how I'm going to get you to come with me."

Caleb tightened the hold on his gun. "I don't think so, buddy. The lady stays with me."

Norman's humor vanished.

"She isn't meant for you," he said, voice pitching low. Threatening.

"And if she was meant for you, you wouldn't have to threaten her into leaving with you," Caleb countered. It clearly angered the man. Caleb realized he should probably tread lightly. It was hard if not downright impossible to read an unstable man. He couldn't tell if Norman was telling the truth or not. "Listen, why don't you disarm your bombs and then we'll talk with Alyssa about leaving with you? I'll even lower my gun."

Norman scrunched up his nose. He made a noise of disgust.

"I'm not falling for any of your tricks," he said. "I know what kind of man you are, Deputy Foster, and I don't trust you." Norman's gaze shifted to Alyssa. "He's a bad man, Alyssa. He's done bad things. You're safer with me."

Caleb clenched his teeth together. Hard. He'd been about to tell Alyssa *everything* a minute before, and now Norman was there ready to spill the beans. How had everything gotten so off track? And where was a deputy or staff member on a smoke break when you needed one?

"If you disarm your bombs, or at the very least let me warn them, I'll come with you."

Caleb kept his hands around the gun but chanced a look at Alyssa.

"I don't think—" he started, but the woman put a hand on his shoulder and squeezed to silence him. She kept her gaze on Norman.

"Do we have a deal?"

The man adjusted his glasses with his free hand, as if he was thinking. He shook his head.

"You come with me and Mr. Foster here can warn whoever he sees fit to warn once we're gone. I won't detonate any of the bombs, but I won't disarm them either. That's not my job," he said. "That's my only offer."

To show he meant it he lifted the phone. His thumb hovered above its keys.

"And where is Dupree?" Alyssa said, no doubt hedging her answer. Though in hindsight Caleb would realize later that, at that moment, she'd already decided. "*I* don't trust him."

"Don't worry about him. He has his orders." Norman returned his gaze to Caleb, but not before checking the watch he was wearing. "Part of those being that he'll use a second detonator if he doesn't hear from me in the next two minutes. So, even if you decided to be a fool and shoot me, the damage would already be done."

"I'll go," Alyssa rushed. "I'll go!"

Caleb was trying his best to figure out a different solution and coming up blank. Or, rather, ending with a *boom*. He'd seen firsthand the destruction left in the wake of Norman's handiwork at Ted's house. So had Alyssa. She wouldn't want that for Robbie and Eleanor.

And neither would Caleb.

But to let Alyssa go with Norman?

"He won't hurt me," Alyssa whispered at his side. "Please, let me go." He was sure Norman heard it, but the man didn't comment. Caleb didn't lower his gun. He looked at Alyssa.

"I don't want to," he said, honestly. He wanted to point out that just because Norman was obsessed with her didn't mean he wouldn't hurt her.

Her blue eyes were an ocean of feeling when she responded.

"We have to protect them. They'd do the same for us." Alyssa gave him the smallest of smiles.

He didn't return it.

"I'll find you," he said instead. Then said to Norman, "And I'll make you pay."

Norman laughed before taking Alyssa's hand. Caleb felt like his heart was burning through his chest as he watched them walk behind the building to the back parking lot. The moment they were out of eyesight, Caleb grabbed his phone and readied to follow them while warning Missy and the Rickmans.

But then he heard a truly chilling sound.

It was Alyssa. And she was screaming. What, he couldn't understand.

Every part of Caleb's body propelled him forward, following the intangible connection between him and Alyssa that had formed over the last few days.

But he didn't make it two steps.

The parking lot exploded around him.

Chapter Twenty-Two

There were no clouds in the sky. Just an endless sea of blue. It reminded him of something, but he couldn't put his finger on it. So he just kept looking up, waiting to remember.

But it never came.

Instead something blocked his view.

It was a man and he was yelling something.

That was when he noticed the ringing in his ears.

And the pain. And the heat. And that the man looking down at him was the sheriff.

And then everything else filtered back in.

"Where's Alyssa?" Caleb yelled, his words a warbling sound. He struggled to get up off the asphalt. Sheriff Reed helped by putting himself under his arm. Caleb let out a howl of pain he didn't have to hear to know. The sheriff in turn quickly switched sides.

"Alyssa?" he repeated as they began to walk.

It was harder than it should have been.

The sheriff's mouth moved, but Caleb couldn't make out any sound that made sense. There was too much ringing and something else.

Caleb turned to look over his shoulder. The side parking lot was engulfed in a blanket of smoke, metal and fire. His car was among them but still recognizable. The car two down, however, was a twist of metal and paint. As far as he could tell, two others in the lot were the same.

Norman hadn't blown up the entire parking lot, just some of the cars.

And it would have been enough to take him out too, if Alyssa had not screamed. But she had, and that was all he'd needed to start running to her.

Even when she was being kidnapped, she'd managed to save him.

The ringing in his head worsened and his vision started to spin. Throbbing pain lit up his shoulder. Maybe he wasn't as good as he had hoped. The world tilted and swayed, but the sheriff guided him inside through the back of the department before his legs gave way.

The sheriff yelled something that sounded like an order. Seconds later a deputy named Brant appeared. He helped walk Caleb to the break room two doors down. It was already filled with people, all sporting varying looks of concern and fear. Cassie was among them. She made her way through the group and pointed toward the couch. The sheriff and Brant dropped him as best they could onto it.

The ringing in Caleb's ears lessened enough to finally make out what the sheriff was trying to ask.

"Where does it hurt?"

Caleb couldn't have thought of a more idiotic question, but in the back of his mind, he knew the man was only trying to help. Still, he had better things to worry about.

"Everywhere," he said, assuming it was more of a yell than anything. "Where's Alyssa?"

The ringing could have been turned on loud and Caleb still wouldn't be distracted from the face the sheriff was making.

"You don't know," Caleb answered himself.

Sheriff Reed shook his head.

"But we'll find her," he promised with a raised voice. "But first—"

He pointed to Caleb's shoulder. Cassie's face pinched. Brant's did too.

"It's dislocated," Caleb guessed. The pain he was feeling was a familiar one, he realized. He'd dislocated it before.

The sheriff nodded. He picked up Caleb's wrist and arm.

"Brace yourself," he yelled. "This is going to hurt."

THE HOUSE WAS MASSIVE, but it was also a shell.

Alyssa felt empty too.

"Stop your whining and pick up the pace," Dupree said at her elbow. "This detour to grab you already wasted enough of my time."

After the explosions, Alyssa had turned into a violent, violent woman. She'd lashed out at her captor as Norman tried his best to push her into the back seat of a car. Dupree had been there, ready. He'd put his hand around her throat and held her until he could slip a pair of handcuffs on her.

Then, when she'd tried to fight again, he'd told her in no uncertain terms that while the bombs with the witnesses had been a bluff, that didn't mean he personally couldn't go out and kill every single one of them.

It was a threat that pierced through her grief and made her quiet. Still, the drive out to the country had become a blank space in her memory. All she could think about was Caleb.

And how she should never have left him.

Dupree pushed her through the main floor, up a set of grand stairs, and stopped at a room with only two chairs inside.

"Where are we?" she had to ask. Her throat hurt, but she'd managed to stop crying. If only for the sheer bizarre situation she was currently in.

"Your house," he said, pushing her farther into the room. He pointed to one of the chairs. It was facing a large, unobstructed window. Green grass and trees stretched out as far as she could see while an enormous deck pushed out from the first floor. It looked over a good-sized swimming pool, covered with a pool tarp.

"I don't understand," she said. "It doesn't look like *anyone* lives here."

"Not yet."

Alyssa felt her skin crawl as Norman's voice entered the room.

"But today we start."

"FOUND IT! MY GOD, I finally found it."

Caleb looked up from his computer as Captain Jones ran into the bull pen. He didn't slow as he made his way through to the conference room where the sheriff had made the base of operations since the station had gone into lockdown three hours beforehand. Just thinking about the time that had gone by and they still didn't have a lead on Norman or Alyssa made Caleb's stomach twist.

But he was starting to like the enthusiasm in the captain's voice.

"What did you find?" the sheriff was already asking by the time he made it into the room. While Caleb's shoulder had been popped back into place, the explosions had covered his body in cuts, burns and pain. All minor compared to what could have been. Still, he'd spent a useless amount of time trying to fend off the advice of the EMTs. He'd go get seen about after he found Alyssa. And only then.

"The briefcase," Jones exclaimed. "And damn if it wasn't hard to track down. But, thanks to the current manager of the bank and the shop across from it, I found the sucker."

He bent over the table to an open laptop. His fingers danced across the keyboard and mouse until he was satisfied. Caleb waited. It was a hard feat.

"Norman goes back to pick it up three weeks after the robbery." He stepped back so they could crowd around the laptop's screen. It was a picture of Norman holding the case they'd seen him enter the bank with earlier. "No one paid him much mind, since no one from the original robbery was actually there that day. Which means, not only did he hide the briefcase before the robbery, he waited until he knew he could go back and get it without being recognized."

"Which means whatever was in that briefcase was extremely important to him," Caleb concluded.

Jones nodded. He held up his index finger.

"But that's not the exciting part," he said. "All the witnesses inside the bank during the robbery told authorities that Dupree and Anna disappeared into the back to go to the vault to fill their bags with money. Even the manager at the time, Davis Palmer, corroborated that story. However, after we made the discovery about the briefcase, I decided to give Davis a call to just go over everything one more time." He smiled. The gesture wasn't born of happiness but excitement. He'd found something. Something important. "While Anna shoveled money into her bag, she ordered Davis to get on his hands and knees and face the corner. He assumed Dupree was always there in the vault with them because a few minutes later he walked Davis and Anna out."

Jones held his finger up again to tell the room to hold on. He moved quickly to the whiteboard and wiped a space clear. He started to draw as he spoke.

"Two days after the robbery the bank owner took stock of all the damage done, making a list to turn over to CSU to add to their findings as well as a copy for insurance."

Caleb took a step closer as the man's drawing began

to look like rough floor plans. The bank's floor plan, to be more precise.

"Two of those items included a busted lock on one door and another door off its hinges." Jones circled two spots on the drawing. According to the floor plan, those doors were separated by a hallway that ran parallel to what Caleb assumed was the vault.

"The owner admitted to the head of CSU that he'd already been having issues with one of the doors being loose." Jones pointed to the one closest to him. "So it wasn't flagged as something suspicious. Just as the busted lock wasn't either, since they'd also had some problems with it sticking before. Plus, it was assumed that Dupree never left the vault until now. The owner and CSU had bigger fish to fry and chalked it up to a coincidence or just moved past it altogether."

Captain Jones tapped the vault, moved his marker to the hallway next to it and moved past another hallway's intersection all the way until he made it to the circle he'd drawn for the busted lock.

"This leads into the safe-deposit room," he said. Before anyone could comment, he ran the marker back down the hallway to the intercepting one. He tapped the second dot he'd drawn for the door off its hinges. "And this is the employees'-only entrance next to the bathrooms and lobby. It's usually always locked."

The captain capped his marker.

Caleb's mind was racing.

"The robbery *was* just a distraction," he said, already going through the implications in his head. "Dupree slips out while Anna keeps the manager occupied.

There's no one to stop him from going to the safe-deposit boxes, so he gets something out of one of them and goes into the bathroom, where he stashes whatever it was into the hidden briefcase. He gets caught, but Norman has no issues coming back a few weeks later and getting it."

"He could easily have hidden it behind a ceiling tile," the captain added. "No one would have looked up there unless there was a reason to. And there's already no cameras in front of the bathrooms."

"But what about the cameras outside the safe-deposit room or in the hallways?" the sheriff asked. "And, for that matter, what about the two keys needed to open one of those boxes?"

The captain didn't look as excited as he once had.

"The cameras covering both had been down a week and a half," he answered. "The owner had called for a technician, but he never showed up. After the robbery he called a different company and they came out to fix it. Again, everyone thought these were separate issues."

"But together they're making a brand-new picture of what happened," Caleb finished. "The sheriff's right, though. Let's say Dupree had one of the keys to get into the box. He still needs the manager's—" The captain's expression stopped Caleb's thoughts. "Let me guess, a set of his keys went missing and no one thought to add that into any kind of report."

Captain Jones nodded.

"Davis admitted he thought he lost his keys during his attempt to escape when the shooting started." Jones's expression softened a fraction. "Not that I give in to rumors around here, but Cassie heard that Davis had been sweet on Larissa Colt. He was with her when she died."

They all silenced.

If Caleb had been in the bank manager's position, holding on to Alyssa while she... Well, he also wouldn't think twice about lost keys. Especially when they didn't appear to have any bearing for what happened.

"Okay," Caleb said, breaking the silence. "If all this is true, then we know *why* the robbery happened but not *what* was taken. Is there any way to find out which box he might have opened?"

Sheriff Reed's expression scrunched in thought. Then he was jumping up out of his chair. "I have an idea."

Caleb listened to the plan with optimism as the sheriff explained it to a roomful of deputies before disappearing altogether. That feeling, however, started to dwindle as another half hour went by. By the time it turned into an hour, he was ready to throw in the towel and start to search all of Riker County inch by inch until he found Alyssa.

But then they finally got something they'd been lacking in the last week.

A good lead.

"We have a caller who claims a file of his is missing from his safe-deposit box," a deputy named Patty said, rushing into the conference room. Caleb jumped up, body stringing up with an adrenaline boost. The sheriff was on her heels.

"Dean Cranston."

No sooner had he read the name out loud than Reed's expression darkened.

"Who's Dean Cranston?" Caleb asked, annoyed he was new to town. "And what's missing?"

"Dean Cranston owns a processing plant on the outskirts of town," Cassie answered. The sheriff cursed beneath his breath. "He isn't the most liked man in Riker County."

"Why?" Caleb once again was in the dark. He didn't like it one bit.

"He inherited the plant when his father passed away a few years ago and decided to make a few changes the county didn't agree with," Patty answered.

"And by changes she means he started outsourcing almost everything he could to cut costs," the sheriff said, clearly angry. "He laid off more than three hundred people and then dumped the extra savings into building a fancy hotel in the city of Kipsy. He's always been in love with his own name and thinks he's some kind of celebrity when really most people just despise him for the greedy man he is. His layoffs forced a lot of longtime residents to move out of the county just to find a job. It ruined a lot of families. It wasn't pretty."

"So this guy is scum," Caleb said. "But what is his connection to Norman and—" He stopped himself and changed gears. A hunch began to yell so loudly he couldn't help blurting it out. "What if Norman was one of those families? What if he was laid off?"

"He said he was out for revenge," the sheriff said, eyes widening. They were finally getting some traction.

"What better target is there than a scumbag employer who took away your livelihood?" Caleb added. The sheriff snapped his fingers.

"But what did he take from the safe-deposit box?" Cassie asked Patty.

The deputy's lips had stretched into a grim line.

"Detailed blueprints to the Cranston Hotel in Kipsy," she said. "And Cranston's secretary relayed this information to me because Cranston was getting ready for a party being thrown tonight in his honor... at the Cranston."

The sheriff and Caleb shared a look.

"It's a lot easier to destroy a building if you know just where to put the bombs," Caleb pointed out.

"And that's one hell of a way to get revenge."

Chapter Twenty-Three

The sunset was beautiful, all things considered.

Alyssa watched through the window as violet, red and orange faded into darkness with a weird sense of calm. Or shock. She didn't care which. All she knew was that she was stranded in a place where fear and anger and anguish had become a constant. And, in that way, they had canceled each other out.

Now she was waiting for an opening.

One she hadn't been able to get, since Norman hadn't left her side in hours. She'd tried to talk to him, to understand what was going on, but he'd told her on repeat to wait for the sunset. She'd contemplated running but knew Dupree was near. She could hear his heavy steps echoing.

"Did you enjoy it?" Norman asked once they were staring at darkness through the window. It made her jump. When she didn't answer he continued, unperturbed. "When I built this house, that's what made me choose this room as my favorite. Sure, all the other views are nice, but there's something about *this* spot that makes it feel magical." He let out a long sigh. His tone changed. "This was supposed to be my castle. I was going to be the king."

He reached over and, as if her hands weren't cuffed behind her, patted the top of the armrest.

"I'm glad you stayed," he said, stronger. "It would have been a shame had you left too. I might be forgiving, but I'm not that forgiving."

Alyssa's emotions were starting to pick up traction again, a slimy feeling along with them. It was like Norman was and wasn't there. Like he was and also wasn't talking to her. She wondered if she could use his struggle with reality to her advantage.

"Who else left?" she asked, careful to keep a soothing tone. Even if she wanted nothing more than to cause his pain. "Norman?"

He lazily moved his gaze to hers.

"She said if I couldn't have a castle, then I couldn't be a king. And she deserved more than someone like me."

His words were low and hollowing out. Alyssa's muscles started to tense. Readying. To run or fight, she didn't know.

"And why could you not have a castle?" she asked, matching his volume. "Isn't that where we are right now?"

A faint smile crossed his lips.

Then it twisted.

"These are just walls," he snarled, getting to his feet. "They don't mean anything, Barbara!" Norman's eyes were crazed when they met hers. Alyssa didn't move an inch. He rounded the chairs and stopped in front of her, grabbing the armrests. Who was Barbara? "We could have been happy, but you left me! Why?"

Alyssa yelled out in surprise as Norman lunged at the chair. Together she flipped over with it. Pain lit up her back as it connected with the hardwood.

"It wasn't my fault he took it all away from us," Norman roared, still rooted in his own world. He turned around and punched the window. Not hard enough to shatter it, but Alyssa didn't miss the blood that blossomed across his knuckles. He paid it no mind. "If you'd just given me some time…"

He sighed and looked down at her. "But *we* can be happy here."

Norman lowered himself into a crouch.

To her surprise, he gave her a smile. It was off, but Alyssa was starting to believe that Norman had finally reached a point of constant unraveling. She just hoped she wasn't with him when he finally went over the edge. He reached out and brushed his knuckles along her cheek. His blood was wet against her skin. She fought the urge to shudder.

"We'll be happy here now that you're mine and not some lowly deputy's. You'll see."

In that moment all Alyssa saw was red.

"I am not yours," she said, teeth bared. "I am not his. I. Am. Mine."

Alyssa swung her left hip around and up, her leg with it. The kick caught Norman off guard. He didn't have time to block as her shoe connected with the side of his head. He let out a strangled yell of pain and fell backward. Alyssa knew an opening when she saw one.

She rolled off the chair and managed to get into a sitting position. From there she got to her feet. The movement was hampered by her cuffed hands, but she wasn't about to let that slow her down. Not wanting to chance Norman getting the upper hand again, Alyssa ran straight for the open door. She paused for a second, trying to listen for a clue as to where Dupree was, but Norman's yell of pain changed to one filled with cursing. She decided she was just going to have to chance it.

Unimaginably glad she'd worn good shoes, Alyssa tore down the hallway toward the stairs. Halfway down them, though, a gunshot over her head made her nearly trip.

"What a pain in the ass," Dupree yelled behind her.

Alyssa screamed as another shot sounded. By the time she hit the first floor, her heart was hammering in her chest.

Run, her mind yelled. *Run!*

She wanted to go down the only familiar path she knew of the house, but it was too long and open for her liking. Instead Alyssa ran through the kitchen and toward the back door.

"Don't shoot her!"

Norman's voice carried through the house just as Alyssa made it to a set of French doors. The seconds it took her to turn around and grab the knob with her bound hands were excruciating.

"I'm done playing these games," Dupree yelled back. He was too close for her comfort. "If you don't want me to kill her, *then stop me*."

Alyssa got the door open and ran outside. She was

on the deck that overlooked the sloping yard and the pool. It reminded her of Gabby's giant deck in Colorado. Which gave her the hope that maybe it was built the same way with an access door at its front used for storage.

Norman and Dupree were still yelling behind her.

She didn't waste any more time.

Trying to run as fast and quietly as she could, Alyssa took the side stairs that ran alongside the deck until she was on a concrete patio that surrounded the pool.

"No," she breathed, rounding the front part of the deck. There was no door. Just stained wood and a life preserver placed in the middle.

"You should have hidden," Dupree yelled into the night air, tearing her own thoughts from her mind. "There's nowhere to do that out here."

Alyssa froze up as footsteps thundered toward her.

"You are not worth this effort." Dupree's face swam into view as he peered over the deck and down at her. He was angry, very much the man she'd seen before he'd shot her in the bank. He lowered his gun. "And I have to say, I'm going to really enjoy repeating history."

The shot exploded through the quiet of the night.

Alyssa braced herself for the end.

But it didn't come. At least, not for her.

Dupree dropped his gun and tipped forward. His weight carried him over the railing so fast that Alyssa hurried backward to get out of the way.

Expecting to find solid ground, she yelled in surprise when she started to fall.

Right into the pool.

Cold water rushed over her as the tarp wrapped around her body. Panic exploded in Alyssa's chest. She tried to move upward, but with her hands behind her back, she floundered. She kicked out viciously, but the tarp countered every move she made to try to make it back to the surface. In the movement her glasses fell off her face.

The already dark world blurred.

A muffled shot sounded overhead, but she didn't have the focus to wonder about it. Not while her lungs were starting to burn.

She was suffocating.

Something hit the water next to her. The chlorine burned her eyes as she tried to focus on what it was, but the tarp created a barrier she couldn't see past.

But then, out of that darkness, a hand found her side. Then another.

She stilled as the tarp was pulled away, lungs on fire.

Then she was being pushed to the surface.

"Breathe," a man commanded at her side as soon as she began to cough and sputter. He repeated his order while moving them to the shallow end of the pool. Alyssa did as she was told, turning her gaze to the blur next to her.

But he was too close to be a blur.

"Caleb!"

The deputy gave her a smile that reached into every part of her body and warmed it. His golden hair was in tangles and he looked a little worse for the wear, but there he was. Alive.

"I thought you were—" she started, already fighting tears. Caleb closed the space between them, interrupting her with a kiss.

"But I'm not," he said after they parted. "I'm right here with you."

Alyssa wanted to stay within the warmth that Caleb seemed to always make her feel, but the reality of where they were set back in.

"You shot Dupree before he could kill me," she realized.

Caleb's expression pinched. "Not exactly."

He guided her to the steps of the pool and waited to explain when they were out of the water. The night air made her cold, but she didn't care. Not when Caleb was with her.

"I heard the gunshots in the house, but I got out here too late," he admitted.

"Then who shot Dupree?"

"Norman did." He walked them onto the grass, away from the pool and deck. Away from Dupree's body. Voices sounded from the house. Caleb didn't flinch, which made her assume he'd had backup this time around. "It's not that surprising if you think about it," he continued. "He wanted to protect you."

A range of emotions crossed Caleb's expression. Some were a mystery. Others weren't.

"And I can't blame him for that," he said with the smallest of smiles.

That warmth within her heated, but she still needed to know what had happened while she was underwater. "Where is he now?"

On cue Norman's wail carried over to them. It was followed by a voice she recognized as the sheriff's.

"After he shot Dupree he turned on me," Caleb explained. "I was able to get his gun away without killing him. Then I went in after you."

That sobered Alyssa.

"Good," she said. "I want him to be able to pay for what he's done."

Caleb nodded. "And he will. Of that the sheriff will make sure."

Alyssa might have been cuffed, soaking wet and mostly blind, but in that moment she felt something she never thought she'd feel.

Closure.

ALYSSA HAD HER head hung over one of the biggest cups of coffee Caleb had ever seen. He watched her from the door of the conference room for a few seconds, marveling at how beautiful she was, before he took a deep breath and sat down next to her.

"I need to tell you something," he jumped in. "Something I should have told you a lot sooner." Alyssa turned to him, eyes widened in surprise. He hoped they wouldn't turn away from him completely when he was done.

"I was a beat cop in Portland when my current partner and I got a call to a town house in the suburbs," he started. "When we got there a neighbor said that he'd called because he had heard this man beating his wife almost every night and couldn't take it anymore. He said the screaming was so loud it woke him up. So we investigated." Normally just thinking about that night would awaken a new surge of anger, but somehow looking into Alyssa's eyes made him feel calm. "Long story short, the wife was pretty bad off but didn't want to press charges. I tried my best to convince her to at least leave for the night, but she kept looking back at her husband, clearly terrified. And that's when he looked at me and said, 'She knows she deserved it.'"

Alyssa sucked in a breath. Caleb took one of his own. "Something in me snapped," he admitted. "I threw one punch and before I knew it my partner was pulling me off the man and he was going to the hospital. And *that's* why I was transferred here. I lost control."

Caleb averted his gaze. He thought he could handle it if Alyssa realized she'd made a mistake in getting close to him, but now the thought wasn't one he wanted to face.

"Caleb, look at me."

A warm hand guided his chin to turn toward her.

"I can't pretend to know what it's like being in law enforcement. To go into dangerous and occasionally heartbreaking situations, forced to see the world at its worst sometimes. But what I do know is that you had the chance to kill a very bad man tonight and no one would have blamed you, and yet you didn't." A small smile pulled up the corners of her lips. It was soft and sweet. Just like her. "You wanted him to face justice, the right way. And because of that decision, that's exactly what's going to happen. What you did in the past is already done. All you can do now is move on and become better for it."

She moved closer, and that smile grew. He welcomed her lips, once more, against his. "Plus, I'm here to tell you that if you were looking for some kind of redemption, I think you more than found it here."

Epilogue

"So, everyone has a pool going on you."

Caleb looked up from his desk and couldn't help grinning. Sheriff Reed had once been a man he didn't understand, but after what they'd been through he was a man Caleb not only respected, but liked. "Oh yeah? What kind of pool?"

"On whether or not you'll stay."

Caleb eyed the clock over the man's shoulder, still grinning.

"I actually just ended my shift," he answered, closing the file on his desk and standing. "So technically I'm leaving."

Reed laughed and followed him as he made his way out to the lobby. His blazer was slung over his shoulder. "How convenient. I'm on my way out too."

It had been three weeks since the night Caleb had thought he'd lost Alyssa. And he hated to think it, but he realized he would have, had Dean Cranston not grown a conscience. He'd sent a list of every employee laid off from his plant, and thankfully Norman Calloway had been the only Norman on the list. From there it had been easy to look up his address out on the cusp of Carpenter. The house he'd built for his wife, Barbara. The house he couldn't afford when he'd been laid off. The sheriff had had the pleasure of talking to Barbara after the arrest. She'd admitted to leaving Norman high and dry when he couldn't accommodate her lifestyle and she never looked back.

According to the psychologist assigned to his case, that was when Norman decided he wanted to gain back the control he'd lost. One night he approached an angry man at the bar and promised him revenge if he helped him steal blueprints from a safe-deposit box Norman knew Cranston used. Dupree had agreed easily. While he wasn't an employee of the plant, his father had been. Their family, like Norman's, was shattered because of it.

However, when he'd bumped into Alyssa at the bank, all the stress of what he was doing finally pushed him into a new reality. One where a woman loved him so much that she cheated death just to stay with him. In the year that followed he worked on his plan, believing it was the last obstacle between them, but at the same time began to devolve. His stability took more hits as parts of his plans backfired.

The sheriff believed that if Norman didn't spend his life in prison, he'd at least spend it in an institution. Far, far away from Riker County.

"What's your bet?" Caleb finally had to ask Reed as they walked out of the building.

"You mean do I think you'll stay in Riker County or go back to Portland?"

"Yeah. Will I stay or go?"

The sheriff was already grinning. They paused on the sidewalk.

"First, answer me this," he said. "What are your plans tonight?"

Caleb felt his eyebrow rise. "Alyssa wants to try out the new Chinese place that opened up off Main. We're meeting Robbie and Eleanor there. Why?"

Reed let out a laugh. "That's why I think you'll stay."

Caleb snorted.

"Because of Chinese food?" he hedged, already knowing exactly what the sheriff meant. However, the man didn't answer. Instead he turned his attention over Caleb's shoulder with a look that was nothing but glee.

"Well, hello, Miss Garner! I do believe that you're going to help me win a bet."

Caleb turned in time to see Alyssa confused. She looked between them.

"A bet?" she repeated.

"Don't worry about it," Caleb jumped in, trying not to laugh. "The sheriff just had too much coffee today."

"Speaking of coffee," she started. "I was hoping to grab a cup from the café before we take Sergeant to the dog park, if that's okay with you?"

"Sounds great to me."

Alyssa beamed.

They said goodbye to the sheriff and parted ways in the parking lot. Caleb slipped his hand in hers as they walked. It was warm and perfect.

While the danger had ceased in the last few weeks,

his feelings for the woman next to him hadn't. So, while the department might be taking guesses at whether or not he was going to stay, Caleb already knew the answer.

"Hey, Reed," he called across the lot, stopping the man before he got into his Bronco. "You've already won the bet!"

The sheriff just laughed.

* * * * *

Look for more books in Tyler Anne Snell's
THE PROTECTORS OF RIKER COUNTY
miniseries in 2018.

And don't miss the previous title in
THE PROTECTORS OF RIKER COUNTY *series:*

SMALL-TOWN FACE-OFF

Available now from Harlequin Intrigue!

Sheriff Flint Cahill can and will endure elements far worse than the coming winter storm to hunt down Maggie Thompson and her abductor.

Read on for a sneak preview of
COWBOY'S LEGACY,
A CAHILL RANCH NOVEL *from*
New York Times *bestselling author*
B.J. Daniels!

SHE WAS IN so fast that she didn't have a chance to scream. The icy cold water stole her breath away. Her eyes flew open as she hit. Because of the way she fell, she had no sense of up or down for a few moments.

Panicked, she flailed in the water until a light flickered above her. She tried to swim toward it, but something was holding her down. The harder she fought, the more it seemed to push her deeper and deeper, the light fading.

Her lungs burned. She had to breathe. The dim light wavered above her through the rippling water. She clawed at it as her breath gave out. She could see the surface just inches above her. Air! She needed oxygen. Now!

The rippling water distorted the face that suddenly appeared above her. The mouth twisted in a grotesque smile. She screamed, only to have her throat fill with the putrid dark water. She choked, sucking in even more water. She was drowning, and the person who'd done this to her was watching her die and smiling.

Maggie Thompson shot upright in bed, gasping

for air and swinging her arms frantically toward the faint light coming through the window. Panic had her perspiration-soaked nightgown sticking to her skin. Trembling, she clutched the bedcovers as she gasped for breath.

The nightmare had been so real this time that she thought she was going to drown before she could come out of it. Her chest ached, her throat feeling raw as tears burned her eyes. It had been too real. She couldn't shake the feeling that she'd almost died this time. Next time…

She snapped on the bedside lamp to chase away the dark shadows hunkered in the corners of the room. If only Flint had been here instead of on an all-night stakeout. She needed Sheriff Flint Cahill's strong arms around her. Not that he stayed most nights. They hadn't been intimate that long.

Often, he had to work or was called out in the middle of the night. He'd asked her to move in with him months ago, but she'd declined. He'd asked her after one of his ex-wife's nasty tricks. Maggie hadn't wanted to make a decision like that based on Flint's ex.

While his ex hadn't done anything in months to keep them apart, Maggie couldn't rest easy. Flint was hoping Celeste had grown tired of her tricks. Maggie wasn't that naive. Celeste Duma was one of those women who played on every man's weakness to get what she wanted—and she wanted not just the rich, powerful man she'd left Flint for. She wanted to keep her ex on the string, as well.

Maggie's breathing slowed a little. She pulled the

covers up to her chin, still shivering, but she didn't turn off the light. Sleep was out of the question for a while. She told herself that she wasn't going to let Celeste scare her. She wasn't going to give the woman the satisfaction.

Unfortunately, it was just bravado. Flint's ex was obsessed with him. Obsessed with keeping them apart. And since the woman had nothing else to do…

As the images of the nightmare faded, she reminded herself that the dream made no sense. It never had. She was a good swimmer. Loved water. Had never nearly drowned. Nor had anyone ever tried to drown her.

Shuddering, she thought of the face she'd seen through the rippling water. Not Celeste's. More like a Halloween mask. A distorted smiling face, neither male nor female. Just the memory sent her heart racing again.

What bothered her most was that dream kept reoccurring. After the first time, she'd mentioned it to her friend Belle Delaney.

"A drowning dream?" Belle had asked with the arch of her eyebrow. "Do you feel that in waking life you're being 'sucked into' something you'd rather not be a part of?"

Maggie had groaned inwardly. Belle had never kept it a secret that she thought Maggie was making a mistake when it came to Flint. Too much baggage, she always said of the sheriff. His "baggage" came in the shape of his spoiled, probably psychopathic, petite, green-eyed, blonde ex.

"I have my own skeletons." Maggie had laughed, although she'd never shared her past—even with Belle—before moving to Gilt Edge, Montana, and opening her beauty shop, Just Hair. She feared it was her own baggage that scared her the most.

"If you're holding anything back," Belle had said, eyeing her closely, "you need to let it out. Men hate surprises after they tie the knot."

"Guess I don't have to worry about that because Flint hasn't said anything about marriage." But she knew Belle was right. She'd even come close to telling him several times about her past. Something had always stopped her. The truth was, she feared if he found out her reasons for coming to Gilt Edge he wouldn't want her anymore.

"The dream isn't about Flint," she'd argued that day with Belle, but she couldn't shake the feeling that it was a warning.

"Well, from what I know about dreams," Belle had said, "if in the dream you survive the drowning, it means that a waking relationship will ultimately survive the turmoil. At least, that is one interpretation. But I'd say the nightmare definitely indicates that you are going into unknown waters and something is making you leery of where you're headed." She'd cocked an eyebrow at her. "If you have the dream again, I'd suggest that you ask yourself what it is you're so afraid of."

"I'm sure it's just about his ex, Celeste," she'd lied. Or was she afraid that she wasn't good enough for Flint—just as his ex had warned her. Just as she feared in her heart.

THE WIND LAY over the tall dried grass and kicked up dust as Sheriff Flint Cahill stood on the hillside. He shoved his Stetson down on his head of thick dark hair, squinting in the distance at the clouds to the west. Sure as the devil, it was going to snow before the day was out.

In the distance, he could see a large star made out of red and green lights on the side of a barn, a reminder that Christmas was coming. Flint thought he might even get a tree this year, go up in the mountains and cut it himself. He hadn't had a tree at Christmas in years. Not since…

At the sound of a pickup horn, he turned, shielding his eyes from the low winter sun. He could smell snow in the air, feel it deep in his bones. This storm was going to dump a good foot on them, according to the latest news. They were going to have a white Christmas.

Most years he wasn't ready for the holiday season any more than he was ready for a snow that wouldn't melt until spring. But this year was different. He felt energized. This was the year his life would change. He thought of the small velvet box in his jacket pocket. He'd been carrying it around for months. Just the thought of it made him smile to himself. He was in love and he was finally going to do something about it.

The pickup rumbled to a stop a few yards from him. He took a deep breath of the mountain air and, telling himself he was ready for whatever Mother Nature wanted to throw at him, he headed for the truck.

"Are you all right?" his sister asked as he slid into

the passenger seat. In the cab out of the wind, it was nice and warm. He rubbed his bare hands together, wishing he hadn't forgotten his gloves earlier. But when he'd headed out, he'd had too much on his mind. He still did.

Lillie looked out at the dull brown of the landscape and the chain-link fence that surrounded the missile silo. "What were you doing out here?"

He chuckled. "Looking for aliens. What else?" This was the spot that their father swore aliens hadn't just landed on one night back in 1967. Nope, according to Ely Cahill, the aliens had abducted him, taken him aboard their spaceship and done experiments on him. Not that anyone believed it in the county. Everyone just assumed that Ely had a screw loose. Or two.

It didn't help that their father spent most of the year up in the mountains as a recluse trapping and panning for gold.

"Aliens. Funny," Lillie said, making a face at him.

He smiled over at her. "Actually, I was on an all-night stakeout. The cattle rustlers didn't show up." He shrugged.

She glanced around. "Where's your patrol SUV?"

"Axle deep in a muddy creek back toward Grass Range. I'll have to get it pulled out. After I called you, I started walking and I ended up here. Wish I'd grabbed my gloves, though."

"You're scaring me," she said, studying him openly. "You're starting to act like Dad."

He laughed at that, wondering how far from the

truth it was. "At least I didn't see any aliens near the missile silo."

She groaned. Being the butt of jokes in the county because of their father got old for all of them.

Flint glanced at the fenced-in area. There was nothing visible behind the chain link but tumbleweeds. He turned back to her. "I didn't pull you away from anything important, I hope? Since you were close by, I thought you wouldn't mind giving me a ride. I've had enough walking for one day. Or thinking, for that matter."

She shook her head. "What's going on, Flint?"

He looked out at the country that ran to the mountains. Cahill Ranch. His grandfather had started it, his father had worked it, and now two of his brothers ran the cattle part of it to keep the place going while he and his sister, Lillie, and brother Darby had taken other paths. Not to mention their oldest brother, Tucker, who'd struck out at seventeen and hadn't been seen or heard from since.

Flint had been scared after his marriage and divorce. But Maggie was nothing like Celeste, who was small, blonde, green-eyed and crazy. Maggie was tall with big brown eyes and long auburn hair. His heart beat faster at the thought of her smile, at her laugh.

"I'm going to ask Maggie to marry me," Flint said and nodded as if reassuring himself.

When Lillie didn't reply, he glanced over at her. It wasn't like her not to have something to say. "Well?"

"What has taken you so long?"

He sighed. "Well, you know after Celeste…"

"Say no more," his sister said, raising a hand to stop him. "Anyone would be gun-shy after being married to her."

"I'm hoping she won't be a problem."

Lillie laughed. "Short of killing your ex-wife, she is always going to be a problem. You just have to decide if you're going to let her run your life. Or if you're going to live it—in spite of her."

So easy for her to say. He smiled, though. "You're right. Anyway, Maggie and I have been dating for a while now and there haven't been any…incidents in months."

Lillie shook her head. "You know Celeste was the one who vandalized Maggie's beauty shop—just as you know she started that fire at Maggie's house."

"Too bad there wasn't any proof so I could have arrested her. But since there wasn't and no one was hurt and it was months ago…"

"I'd love to see Celeste behind bars, though I think prison is too good for her. I can understand why you would be worried about what she will do next. She's psychopathic."

He feared that that maybe was close to the case. "Do you want to see the ring?" He knew she did, so he fished it out of his pocket. He'd been carrying it around for quite a while now. Getting up his courage? He knew what was holding him back. Celeste. He couldn't be sure how she would take it—or what she might do. His ex-wife seemed determined that he and Maggie shouldn't be together, even though she was apparently happily married to local wealthy business-man Wayne Duma.

Handing his sister the small black velvet box, he waited as she slowly opened it.

A small gasp escaped her lips. "It's beautiful. *Really* beautiful." She shot him a look. "I thought sheriffs didn't make much money?"

"I've been saving for a long while now. Unlike my sister, I live pretty simply."

She laughed. "Simply? Prisoners have more in their cells than you do. You aren't thinking of living in that small house of yours after you're married, are you?"

"For a while. It's not that bad. Not all of us have huge new houses like you and Trask."

"We need the room for all the kids we're going to have," she said. "But it is wonderful, isn't it? Trask is determined that I have everything I ever wanted." Her gaze softened as the newlywed thought of her husband.

"I keep thinking of your wedding." There'd been a double wedding, with both Lillie and her twin, Darby, getting married to the loves of their lives only months ago. "It's great to see you and Trask so happy. And Darby and Mariah... I don't think Darby is ever going to come off that cloud he's on."

Lillie smiled. "I'm so happy for him. And I'm happy for you. You know I really like Maggie. So do it. Don't worry about Celeste. Once you're married, there's nothing she can do."

He told himself she was right, and yet in the back of his mind, he feared that his ex-wife would do something to ruin it—just as she had done to some of his dates with Maggie.

"I don't understand Celeste," Lillie was saying as she shifted into Drive and started toward the small Western town of Gilt Edge. "She's the one who dumped you for Wayne Duma. So what is her problem?"

"I'm worried that she is having second thoughts about her marriage to Duma. Or maybe she's bored and has nothing better to do than concern herself with my life. Maybe she just doesn't want me to be happy."

"Or she is just plain malicious," Lillie said. "If she isn't happy, she doesn't want you to be, either."

A shaft of sunlight came through the cab window, warming him against the chill that came with even talking about Celeste. He leaned back, content as Lillie drove.

He was going to ask Maggie to marry him. He was going to do it this weekend. He'd already made a dinner reservation at the local steak house. He had the ring in his pocket. Now it was just a matter of popping the question and hoping she said yes. If she did… Well, then, this was going to be the best Christmas ever, he thought and smiled.

* * * * *

Don't miss COWBOY'S LEGACY,
available December 2017
wherever HQN Books and
ebooks are sold.

www.Harlequin.com

#1755 GUNFIRE ON THE RANCH
Blue River Ranch • by Delores Fossen
DEA agent Theo Carter was a suspect in his parents' murder...and now he's back to protect the family he never knew he had.

#1756 SAFE AT HAWK'S LANDING
Badge of Justice • by Rita Herron
Charlotte Reacher is no stranger to the trauma her students have experienced, and as she's the only witness to a human-trafficking abduction, FBI agent Lucas Hawk will have his work cut out for him keeping her safe.

#1757 WHISPERING SPRINGS
by Amanda Stevens
This high school reunion was a shot at redemption and maybe a second chance for former army ranger Dylan Burkhart and his old flame Ava North. But a secret-telling game turns up a murder confession, with the killer hiding among them...

#1758 RANGER PROTECTOR
Texas Brothers of Company B • by Angi Morgan
After Megan Harper is framed for a fatal shooting, protecting her becomes Texas Ranger Jack McKinnon's sole mission...until unspoken desire gets in the way.

#1759 SOLDIER'S PROMISE
The Ranger Brigade: Family Secrets • by Cindi Myers
Different circumstances brought officer Jake Lohmiller and undercover Ranger Brigade sergeant Carmen Redhorse to a cult encampment in Colorado, but teaming up might be their only shot at saving their families... and each other.

#1760 FORGOTTEN PIECES
The Protectors of Riker County • by Tyler Anne Snell
To say Riker County detective Matt Walker and journalist Maggie Carson have bad blood is an understatement. But when the last twenty-four hours of her memory go missing and she gets caught in someone's crosshairs, the lawman who hates her may be her only salvation...

Get 2 Free Books,
Plus 2 Free Gifts—
just for trying the Reader Service!

Everyone worked through grief differently.

Some people started a new hobby; some people threw themselves into the gym.

Others investigated unsolved murders in secret.

"And why, of all people, would you need me here?" Matt asked, cutting through her mental breakdown of him.

Instead of stepping backward, utilizing the large open space of her front porch, she chanced a step forward.

"I found something," she started, straining out any excess enthusiasm that might make her seem coarse. Still, she knew the detective was a keen observer. Which was why his frown was already doubling in on itself before she explained herself.

"I don't want to hear this," he interrupted, his voice like ice. "I'm warning you, Carson."

"And it wouldn't be the first time you've done so," she countered, skipping over the fact he'd said her last name like a teacher getting ready to send her to detention. "But right now I'm telling you I found a lead. A real, honest-to-God lead!"

The detective's frown affected all of his body. It pinched his expression and pulled his posture taut. Through gritted teeth, he rumbled out his thoughts with disdain clear in his words.

"Why do you keep doing this? What gives you the right?" He took a step away from her. That didn't stop Maggie.

"It wasn't an accident," she implored. "I can prove it now."

Matt shook his head. He skipped frustrated and flew right into angry. This time Maggie faltered.

"You have no right digging into this," he growled. "You didn't even know Erin."

"But don't you want to hear what I found?"

Matt made a stop motion with his hands. The jaw she'd been admiring was set. Hard. "I don't want to ever talk to you again. Especially about this." He turned and was off the front porch in one fluid motion. Before he got into his truck he paused. "And next time you call me out here, I won't hesitate to arrest you."

And then he was gone.

Don't miss
FORGOTTEN PIECES
available January 2018 wherever
Harlequin® Intrigue books and ebooks are sold.

www.Harlequin.com

HIEXP1217

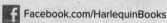

THE WORLD IS BETTER WITH

Romance

Harlequin has everything from contemporary, passionate and heartwarming to suspenseful and inspirational stories.

Whatever your mood,
we have a romance just for you!

Connect with us to find your next great read,
special offers and more.

f /HarlequinBooks

🐦 @HarlequinBooks

www.HarlequinBlog.com

www.Harlequin.com/Newsletters

⬧ HARLEQUIN®

A *Romance* FOR EVERY MOOD™

www.Harlequin.com

SERIESHALOAD2015